THE BLOCK

by
Stefan Draughon

EGIBOOKS
NEW YORK, NEW YORK

THE BLOCK
Copyright © 2019 by Stefan Draughon
All rights reserved.

No part of this book may be reproduced or transmitted in any form or by any means, electronic or mechanical, including photocopying, recording, or by any information storage and retrieval system without the written permission of the author, except where permitted by law. This is a work of fiction. The characters, incidents and dialogue are either drawn from the author's imagination or are used fictitiously, and are not to be construed as real. Any resemblance to actual events or persons, living or dead, is entirely coincidental.

First Edition.

egibooks
P.O. Box 20432
New York, NY 10011
www.egibooks.com

ISBN (print): 978-0-9996699-3-8
ISBN (e-book): 978-0-9996699-8-3

Original Art: Stefan Draughon
Cover Design: Stefan Draughon & Nellie Beavers
E-pub Design: Nellie Beavers

*To
Jozsef, Olive, & Betty*

Table of Contents

1. The Block 11

2. Jimmy and I 17

3. Blue Jeans on the Stoop 29

4. Sweet Sixteen 41

5. Beside the River 51

6. The Little Brown Gabardine Skirt 59

7. Cathy in D.C. 85

8. Mrs. Mann 97

9. Uniforms and Hollywood 111

10. A Trinket from China 127

11. The Accordion 155

Acknowledgements 167

About the Author 169

THE BLOCK

The Scene

This collection of short stories is set within a single block of an ethnically diverse, working-class neighborhood in Yorkville during post-WWII Manhattan.

In one generation, the characters unknowingly lose the inescapable intimacy of their community.

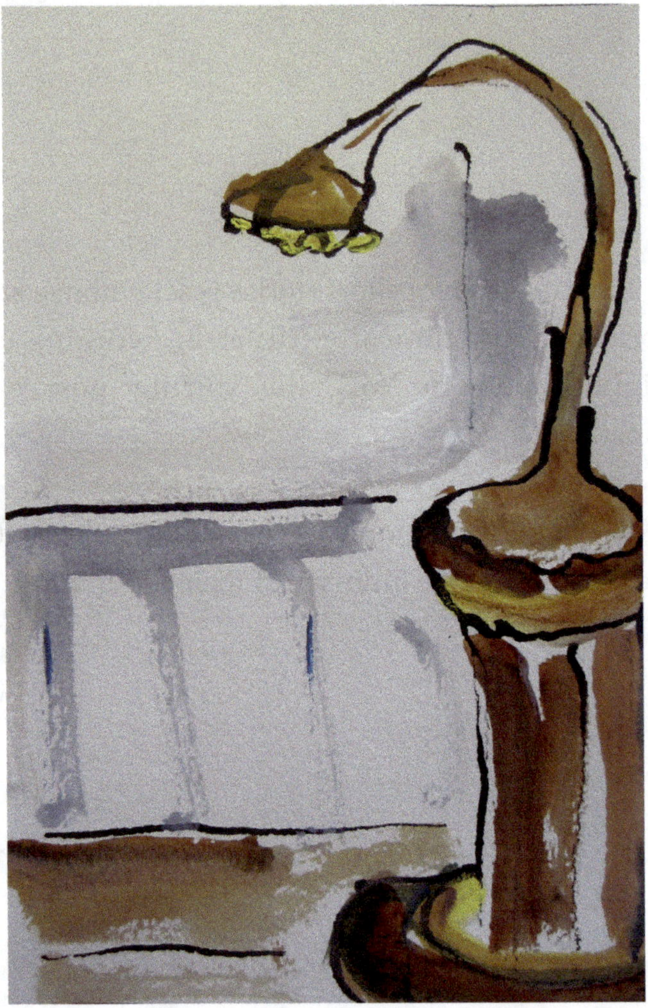

1. The Block

The brownstone stoop had four steep steps. On both sides, along the steps, was a wide railing made of the same claylike concrete as the steps. At the sidewalk level, the railing ended in a pillar form on each side. This particular brownstone stoop was right under a large decorative street lamp with a similar design. The lamppost was home base for "hide and seek," which all the children played virtually every night during the summer.

Living in apartments without air-conditioning, people spent many late nights outside. Not only the children were there, but their parents and neighbors

THE BLOCK

as well. This whole block-life formed a part of the identity of each person living there. Yes, there were also neighborhoods of perhaps four or five square blocks in the city. But the deeper identity of each child and adult was that of the block, their block, quite different from what was around the corner.

Adults brought chairs to sit on during the particularly hot nights. But the kids, when they were not running around, would sit on the stoop steps. Sometimes they rested, sometimes they played house. But as time went on, and they became teenagers, their stoop constituted a meeting place for them to talk with each other. They still played sitting games, they told jokes, but increasingly, they talked to each other.

Now, when I say "block," I don't necessarily mean both sides of the street. Because across the street lived a few kids who were different from the rest of us, not of the block. They were rich and went to private schools. One was very wealthy. On the "block" side of the street, my side of the street, we were working-class Catholic kids mostly.

But that's where the similarity ends. We were as different from each other as we were from the kids across the street. Those differences increased with time. Yes, with "urban renewal" some families moved away from the block. Others just changed and grew differently with time, education, and experience so that, by the time they were eighteen or twenty, each child lived in a different world.

On this block, none of the families had many children, perhaps one or two. They were poor and they were careful.

This story focuses on families from different cultural backgrounds including Hungarian Catholic, English Protestant, as well as Slovakian, Irish, German and Italian Catholics. Several families lived in adjacent brownstones while the others were farther down the block.

Historically, I guess that's the right word, the neighborhood was Hungarian. That meant that around the corner there were many Hungarian restaurants and, in the other direction, there was a butcher, the bookstore, a church, Catholic, another church, Reformed. People walking on the street regularly could be heard speaking Hungarian to each other, without any sense of their being uncomfortable or out of place.

THE BLOCK

All that changed once the developers came in, tore down the brownstones, the Garden restaurants facing their large backyards, the local bakery shop, and destroyed everything on a human scale. Instead they built tall, square, block-long apartment buildings which were, without exception, unaffordable to those who had lived there before. In fact, they were overpriced, even for others who might want to move into such a place. Spaces remained empty for years, despite offers of three-months-free rent a year. It wasn't just that nobody wanted to live there. Nobody who lived there before, wanted to live that way. But that's getting ahead of the story

This all sounds almost idyllic. But the world, even the very small world of this block, was far from heaven. Just one block north and one block east, the children's experiences were very different. One was murdered. Another was a murderer. The poorest children were never given the opportunity to be children at all — to lead even ordinarily stressful lives.

Getting back to the stoop, and the many occurrences there, one in particular stays with me.

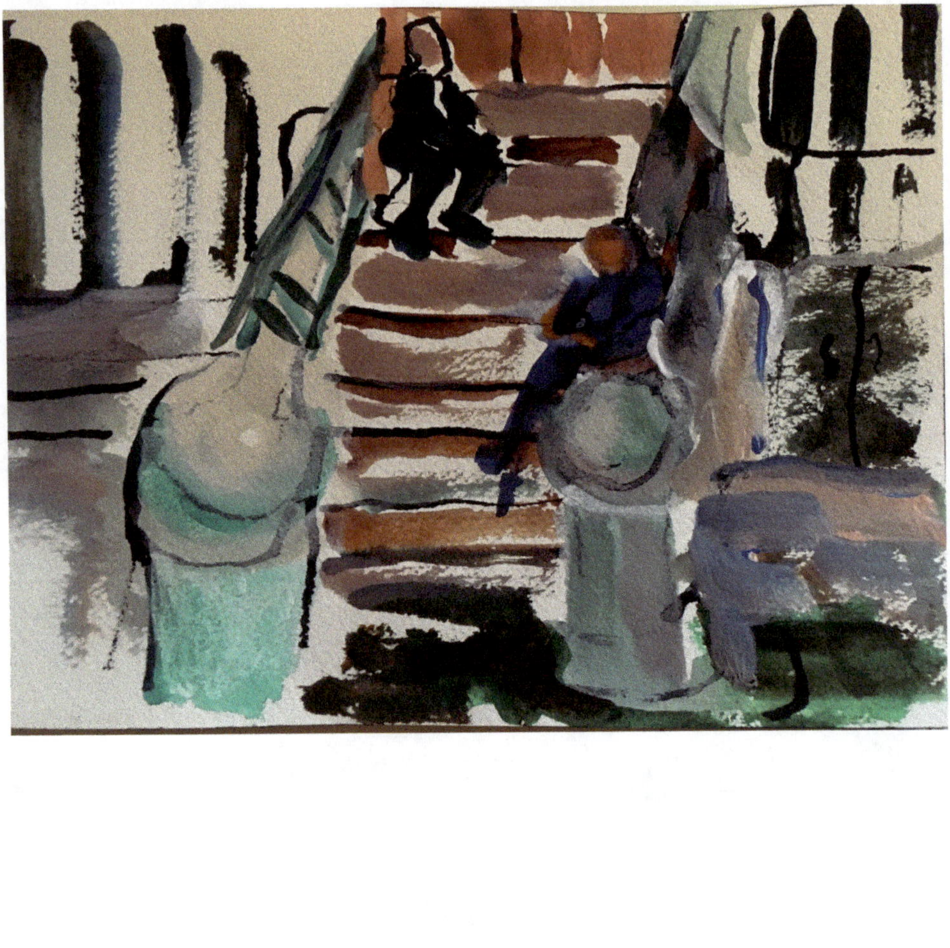

2. Jimmy and I

Jimmy and I were the last ones to be out that evening. He lived right next door to me. As you already know, this is very near the street lamp. I was comfortably placed in the crook of the handrail and pillar at the end of the stoop. He was sitting on an upper step near the doorway of his house, the house with the stoop.

The others had left already. Or maybe there weren't any others. I don't fully remember. But he and I got to talking—talking about relationships between boys and girls, talking about going to college, talking about what we wanted in our lives. Talking about serious things. Things that we both cared about,

THE BLOCK

although we were coming from very different positions with regard to them.

I had pretty much tread the careful path, toeing the line. Doing what people wanted me to do, being a good girl. For me, college was an expected consequence of finishing high school. Although, since we were poor, my family would need me to win a scholarship or go to a public college. But that was a couple years in the future. Not right now. Now, I was most immediately concerned about being attractive to boys. Not that I neglected my studies. I paid them their due. I might not be the best in the class, but I maintained an overall A- average and allowed myself other activities that meant a great deal to me in my life. At the time, that meant dancing at least fifteen hours a week.

Jimmy's path was by no means direct, nor linear and headed straight for college. Three years before this, who would've thought he was going to college? Instead, people on the block thought he probably might wind up in jail. Not that he was threatening or hurtful to anybody. But he had a marked—what should I call it? He had a mischievous, energetic nature. He might take an apple from the grocer's shelf. Or go with some of his friends and get into a fight, a brawl between them and the Irish kids on the next block. After all he was proud of his English heritage and felt he had to defend himself against slurs to his background. In any case, with these minor offenses, he got involved with the police. Unfortunately, not the rock group that came along later.

In the 1950's, the relationship between the kids on the block and the police was not an unfriendly one. I would say that it was cautiously friendly. Not because we were afraid of them, but because sometimes the boys and girls committed minor transgressions like playing ball in the street, or parking a bicycle where it shouldn't be, or bouncing a ball against the wall of the store whose owner didn't necessarily like that.

Jimmy didn't hang out with our group very much, partially because of what I've just described, and partially because he was Protestant, and everyone else was Catholic. But mainly because he was a few years older than we were and seemed to have had more life experience than any of us. He certainly had more experience with the outside world. And he definitely had more experience with girls than I could ever have had the opportunity to have with boys.

THE BLOCK

I think I had a bit of a crush on Jimmy, particularly after his sister's birthday party, when we all played spin the bottle. That was somehow permitted. Parents didn't talk about it, but, in such a big group, and since there was no privacy in a railroad flat, kissing was somehow an acceptable "unacceptable" behavior. At some parties. At some people's houses.

Once spun, there was no way of predicting where the bottle would land. The bottle was set on the floor in the middle of the circle of kids and spun by one person. The person of the opposite sex nearest the direction of the narrow end of the bottle, the pointed end of the bottle, would be the kissing partner. Sometimes there was just one kiss. Other times the couple could stand in the adjacent room to kiss, perhaps behind a French door with clear glass panes in it.

Maybe because of his experience, or maybe because I was more precocious than I had thought I was when it came to boys, when I kissed Jimmy, it was different from kissing the other boys. So, maybe that's part of why I had a crush on him. It was really nice kissing him. I didn't have fantasies about what would happen later on with him—marriage or anything like that. No. Marriage was a long way off, and we were not dating. I just liked talking to him.

Somehow the topic came up about what boys feel is attractive in a girl. And, given the openness and intelligence of the conversations that I had with Jimmy, it was possible to say to him that I was very uncomfortable and felt unattractive because of my skin being all broken out. I mean seriously broken out. I think it was the first time that I ever admitted that to a boy. Yes, I'm sure that was the first time. If he hadn't been a few years older than me and had his own shady past, about which he was open with me, I probably couldn't have mentioned it.

One evening, the issue came up between us that one of the girls in the next house to Jimmy's, and two houses down from where I lived, had become the object of talk. People felt she was "easy" with the boys and were concerned that she might get into trouble. She was all alone with her drunken and abusive parents. Grossly unloved and neglected. Given that kind of treatment for a long time, she became hard. Hard girls were not necessarily easy with boys. But she had no other interests and was not very bright, so it was difficult for her to connect with anybody except in the ways that she knew, which had

THE BLOCK

nothing to do with her mind, and everything to do with her emerging body.

I thought that because boys wanted to have sex with her, this meant that boys found her attractive. I wasn't sleeping with anybody. There was no possibility, not the remotest possibility, that I would be. Although he was different from the other kids on the block, Jimmy never capitalized on being older or on having been in trouble with his minor delinquent experiences. He simply pulled into himself when he was near home. This made our conversations more precious and much more unusual.

Because a kind man took Jimmy under his wing and became his counselor at the Police Athletic League, he was given a scholarship to a private high school, a prep school, out of the neighborhood. Jimmy was bright and ambitious and could work hard. Since he did well in prep school, he won a scholarship to a distant college with free tuition. He concurrently worked part time, as well as attended school, and would continue to do so.

As I thought back on whether he had expressed any interest in me, I became confused. I thought the "hard girl" was really grown up and that that must be what boys like.

I mean, that's what I thought. He listened to what I said. He always did listen and hear. And his response was not what I thought it would be. I thought he would just ignore the whole thing. But instead he started talking about what boys looked for in a girl, particularly in terms of what they wanted from that particular "hard girl." And he explained the difference between a boy wanting to just have sex, without talking to them, perhaps without sharing any words at all. Without being friends or being in any way a romantic lover. Without having a relationship with someone whom he loved and wanted to become more intimate with emotionally, not just physically. In the years that followed, I learned what it was like to sleep with someone and have nothing to say to them in the morning. One relationship like that was enough to teach me the accuracy of what Jimmy had said that night.

But he said more. He said that—and this was clearly directed to me—he said that being able to talk with someone was sometimes being closer than having sex with them at that moment. Being able to be friends with someone was a wholly different

THE BLOCK

experience, and a very important one. And then he talked directly to me. He said he saw that I was capable of having a meaningful, intelligent conversation and also capable of being a friend. That, in the long run, yes, that would get me a lot further in life than just being a magnet for boys who only wanted to lay them and then leave right away.

He was not at all coming on or leading me on. He was telling me something that he sincerely believed, something that I came to be able to believe, because of who was saying it, and because of the context in which we were talking.

This conversation changed my view of myself. I felt as if I really had something to offer people, and specifically to a boy, to a man in my life. I still remember our talk. I remember our then sitting in comfortable silence for a long while.

I thanked him for what he had helped me see. I certainly felt that. What a gift this conversation had been, especially because he was going away, far away from my point of view at that time. My view of the world was not as large as the one I later came to envision.

Yes, he was leaving in a few days to go to college, four hundred miles away in a small town. It was a huge step for him. And if he hadn't been saved by the counselor, one particular person who had believed in him several years before, I could swear that this conversation never would have happened, that he'd never be going off to college. Didn't matter how bright he was. It never would have entered his dreams, let alone his plans for his life.

He had quit school in the eighth grade. Never even finished high school. And without this counselor, who'd had faith in Jimmy, who had tutored him, helped him when he went back to school, who managed to get him a scholarship to a private high school so that he wouldn't have to be exposed to the same group that got him into trouble the first time around, his future would have been different. The prep school was close-by, but not in the neighborhood. It was a wholly different group of people, a private school with students of differing socioeconomic levels. The students wore a uniform, but it was a preppy kind of uniform. And he never capitalized on it. Any more than he had capitalized on his difficulties as a kid going for counseling.

THE BLOCK

Perhaps the fact that someone was able to help him and counsel him, perhaps because he had been given that gift in his life, he was able to give to me. Not the same gift. But the gift of honoring myself and believing in a future that was better than anything imaginable at the moment. I never thought that before, or understood how much he had given me that night. It would last me throughout my life. I had a future as a woman. He had a future as a man. A man making a contribution, in whatever way he could, to the world he lived in and to other people.

I saw him only once again in my life and that's when his sister died of leukemia. Dead before she was eighteen years old. She was the first person of our age group to die. It was incredibly shocking and jolting to each of us in our own way. No matter how hard he had tried to protect his sister from the things that he knew about which could have hurt her, cancer was something he had no control over. He couldn't even stop the boy she was engaged to, her fiancé, from coming to her hospital room, as soon as she was admitted, and asking for his engagement ring back.

At the funeral of Jimmy's eighteen-year-old sister, who had been killed in society by yet a different kind of threat, he seemed more detached than ever. He'd been away at college three years by that time. Other than saying hello, or nodding across her grave, there was no communication between Jimmy and me again. By then, I was married for the first time. But I remember our conversation as clearly as if it were yesterday, not decades ago. And it is strange, but probably not strange at all, that when I sat down to write about this remote, yet pivotal, moment where my soul began its journey, my story came to life. It became real.

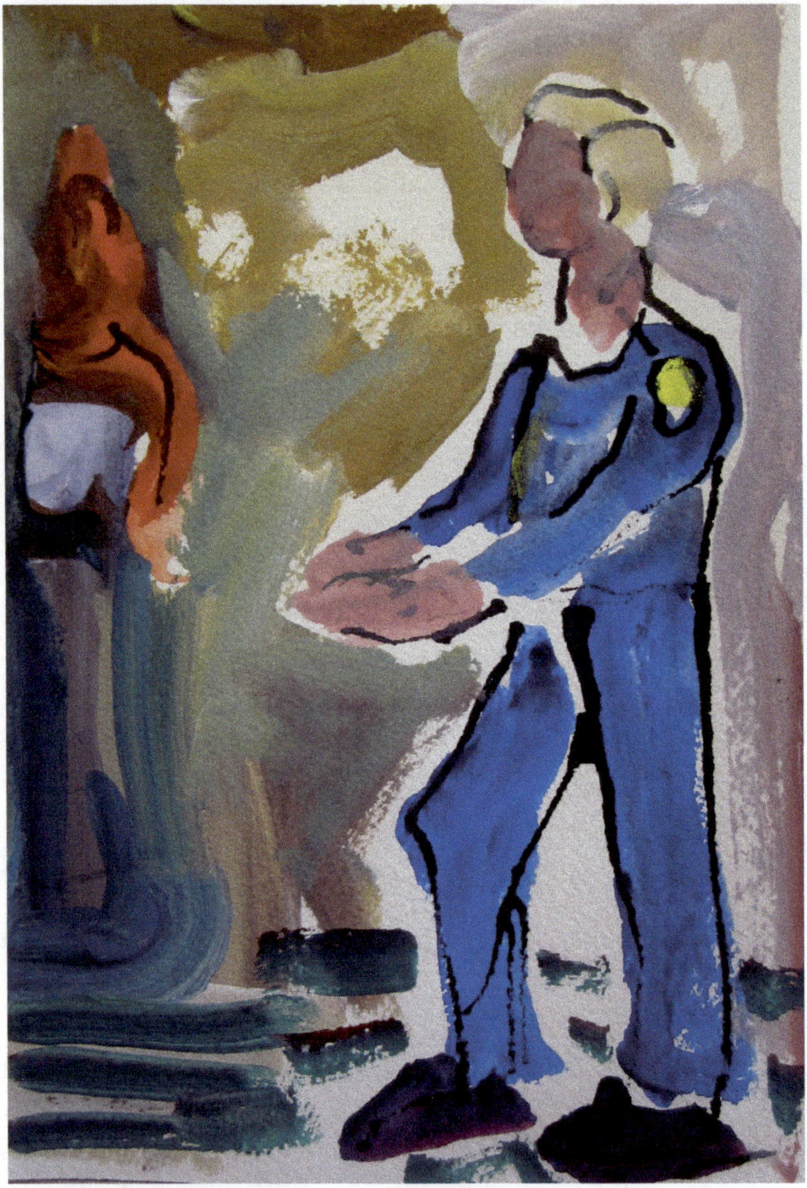

3. Blue Jeans on the Stoop

Fireworks were not really legal in Manhattan. But, like the numbers game, they somehow managed to be present year after year. A few boys on the block would make their way to Jersey, buy the fireworks, and proudly present them to the rest of us on the block each Fourth of July around eight o'clock in the evening.

It was too light then to set them off, but everyone came out of their homes and made themselves comfortable to celebrate the holiday as a community. The celebration included firecrackers, a cherry bomb

THE BLOCK

or two, an explosive that, once lit, traveled on the ground in an unpredictable pattern before exploding (crudely called "ass chasers" by the boys among themselves in the early Fifties). And lots and lots of sparklers.

Then there were the Roman candles which lit up the sky. Not really the sky, but the buildings across the street with brightly-colored, patterned sparks shooting straight up or spreading out in a fan-like shape. Sometimes, at the peak of their display, a firecracker or two went off.

I'm not sure how these were paid for. Remember that most of them, possibly all of them except the sparklers, were not legal in the city, so price gouging was not unreasonable to expect. That did not preclude people, sometimes kids, sometimes adults, and sometimes the kids supervised by the adults, from exploding them, making their own show on the evening of the Fourth of July.

Partially because of the expense, and partially because this group of boys on the block were basically cautious, raised by generally religious immigrant parents, the show was small potatoes and had proceeded for years without anyone trying to stop them. Should someone see potential untoward behavior suggestive of intent to harm anyone, a parent, actually any adult, would intervene. As with baby bats reared by the community of bats, these kids obeyed all the adults, regardless of whether they were parents or not. Still, I never saw an instance of harm.

Yet, personally, I was terrified of fireworks, and even felt uncomfortable holding a lit sparkler. I could hold it, though, because I knew it wouldn't explode and hurt me or anybody else. The firecrackers were troublesome but mild compared to the cherry bombs. Those were loud and the major source of injury to children and adults, especially if they were thrown randomly anywhere near people. Fortunately, they were expensive and usually only one or two were carefully exploded that night. The focus was on the Roman candles, with an occasional firecracker.

As you can imagine, all of us kids were sitting on the stoop, first awaiting the displays and the noise, and then watching them go off. I was seated on the railing at the end, against the pillar, and was wearing my newly hand-me-down blue jeans from my aunt. The other girls were casually dressed, some in jeans and some in skirts. And the four boys were all in jeans.

THE BLOCK

The time did come when the explosions were announced to begin in earnest. Just moments after that, the siren of a police car joined in the noise. The boys who were holding the explosives became panicky. They knew that what they were doing was against the law. Since they had been caught doing small things in the past that had gotten them into trouble, like riding a bike on the sidewalk, they were sincerely afraid, not just that they would be arrested, but also that their dearly held and carefully acquired stash of fireworks would be confiscated by the police.

Other than the usual cop on the beat, whom everyone knew, the police were not a habitual presence. So, the emerging police car was a most uncommon sight. The boys became fidgety and nervous. Couldn't figure out where to hide the fireworks. Trash cans? No. They would be searched. As would the boys' pockets and clothes.

The boys decided that the girls should hide the firecrackers on their person, in their pockets, and then deny any knowledge of their existence or how they had gotten there. Asked by the police, they knew nothing. The police would not search the girls unless they could justify it, with a good reason. They were scared of being charged with molestation of a juvenile. All remembered that one of these girls had been molested at school by a stranger a couple years before. So this group, both police and kids, was particularly sensitive on the issue.

The car stopped right in front of our stoop. A policeman came out and questioned everyone in general. The boys in particular. One after another, each boy was searched and found clean. The girls individually and collectively all denied that they had seen any firecrackers that evening. The policeman, though naturally skeptical, accepted their statements and did not search them. Of course, they did search the trash cans, and the hallway, and the basement entrance and steps, just in case.

As the policeman returned to the car, he yelled a warning to us on the stoop. He would be back later that evening to make sure everyone was okay. The car lights came back on. That same car moved down the street toward the next batch of kids who had their own plans for the Fourth.

Once the car was out of sight, the girls quickly removed the firecrackers from their pockets and gave them back to the boys. The relief that each of them felt was palpable. The girls because they could relax and

THE BLOCK

be less scared both of the police and of the danger they'd been in while the fireworks were on their person. The boys were relieved that they hadn't been taken by the police and that their precious fireworks were now safely back in their possession.

All this took place in probably five minutes, but it felt like a long time. That was how long it took then. Then, there was how long it felt then, which was at least an hour. But there is also how long such a memory can last. It can last a lifetime.

How come? Nobody was ostensibly hurt. It had turned out okay. Right? But, in hindsight, what if somehow one of those firecrackers had gone off? Normally, they didn't by themselves. But sometimes, especially since the quality control was poor, they could just explode. If that had happened, the girl could have been seriously hurt. Not only scarred, but even conceivably hurt inside. Maybe never be able to have a child. Yet, cavalierly, each of us sought to save face. Yes. And at the same time, to enact the then-acceptable girl-and-boy roles. Boys were aggressive, took charge and took risks. Girls followed the boys' lead, even to the point where they could endanger themselves.

No one seriously questioned this. The programming was already solidly set in place.

Boys could justify their putting the girls at risk by thinking that such spontaneous explosions are very rare. Or that everyone knew that the girls wouldn't be searched. The police would not even accuse them of lying. After all, these were "good" girls. Most went to Catholic school or certainly were brought up in working-class, morally concerned families.

***

Out of the blue, and looking back, I remembered that just a few years before the fireworks, I'd been having dinner with my parents and some new acquaintances who lived outside the city. There, dinner was done differently from at home. I was used to the three of us, my parents and I, always eating dinner together, no matter how late my father had to work. I had never seen what then was occurring right before my eyes at that dinner.

Women, of course, cooked the food in the kitchen —the no man's land. Then it was carefully placed in large bowls and platters and brought to the table by the women. All the men, and only the grown men,

THE BLOCK

sat down on the chairs around the table. They began to eat right away. None of the women sat down with them, or ate with them. Obviously, the children were also excluded and remained with their mothers. No. Not everyone was an invited guest at that moment.

Once the men had finished eating, they rose from the table, stepped outside to talk the talk of working-class men. Topics ranged from the food, to their work, or even to playing cards. A few went off to play chess. While this was going on, the women, who had remained inside the house, began to occupy the chairs at the table that were emptied when the men left. True, each new occupant had a fresh plate, as did each of the children seated near mother. They all talked at the table. About the food, about the weather, about children, about their own aches and pains and pregnancies.

Not one woman questioned what seemed so odd to me. How come everyone didn't eat together? Why this segregated strange way of living? It was so unlike what I was used to at home. Was there just not enough room at the table for everyone? No. There was plenty of room. And the kids loved being squeezed in between adults and feeling they were a part of it all. Part of the party. Touched and loved. Included as people.

***

So, yes! Certainly, on the Fourth of July, the girls put the firecrackers into their pockets. It was only natural to do that. Only natural for girls to obey and to take the risk. Would I comply today? I'd like to think I would say, "Not on your life." I'd surely refuse. But if everyone complied, might I not follow their lead?

After years of living, and thinking about that, one day the answer to my question came. It came when I least expected it. In the place where I least expected it. In church.

As a young adult during mass, specifically the second part of the mass, the offering of the Eucharist, I saw everyone around me kneeling at one point. Up until that part of the mass, there had been only brief kneeling, mostly sitting and standing. But when everyone was kneeling, I said to myself, "The priest isn't kneeling." He honors and respects God. Why must I kneel? The God I believe in would not want me on my knees. Not on my knees for him. He didn't

THE BLOCK

need that reassurance or submission. Respect, yes. Honor, yes. But kneeling? I don't think so.

I remained standing while everyone else kneeled. I was nervous. Would I be ostracized afterwards? I was nervous, too, that in some people's minds, I was offending God. Yet, in my mind I was closer to God than I had ever felt in my heart, and in my life. Like Moses, now I could talk to God this way, one-to-one. Have a conversation, however internal and solitary that might seem to others. And the miracle was that each person could do this, even all at the same time, because that conversation was really a conversation with God in each of us

I felt whole. Became a whole person with self-respect. As I walked out of the church, no one said anything. It was as if no one had noticed. I never found out whether they had or hadn't. But gradually, week by week, one person after another stood as well. In some churches today, virtually everyone stands.

I had stood alone that day and survived. Not just surviving, but thriving in my relationship with the mass, with prayer, and with the priests in the church with whom, then, somehow the possibility of friendship emerged between us, where it had never been before. They were human beings. I was, too. They were flawed. When we talked as equals, they could be open about their flaws and doubts, their concerns. They, too, had mothers who were ill. They had financial problems. They were lonely.

But mostly, they had doubt. They had deep faith. But there is no faith without doubt. They go hand in hand. Faith implies a leap into the unknown or unknowable. Otherwise there is certainty. Certainty does not go hand-in-hand with doubt. Or with faith.

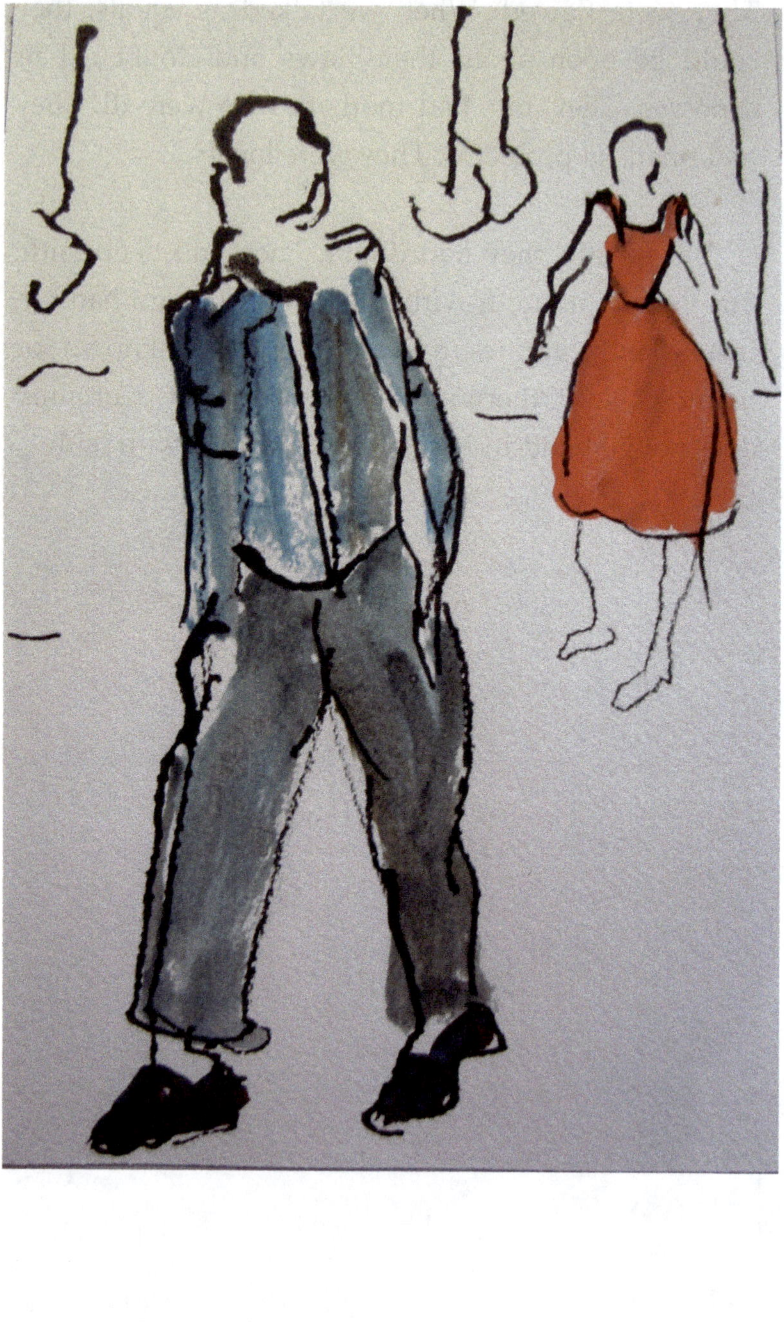

4. Sweet Sixteen

I was surprised that Julia had invited me to her sixteenth birthday party. When we were very little, we had been friends with each other, in a distant kind of way, brought together by the proximity of where we lived. But not necessarily at all, by the things that our families shared — or that we, as children, shared.

However, we were from two Hungarian families and, during World War II, that was sufficient reason to bring us together, at least a little bit. No more than three enemy aliens were permitted to gather in public. Hungarians were technically on the other side. It is true, we two girls were the same age. Both only children. Both living in working-class apartments on

THE BLOCK

the edges of East Harlem. But we were different as night from day.

I don't remember what kinds of games we played, if any. But one visit to Julia's house remains in my memory. And I have no idea why it does, except that what we did was a bit odd. While our mothers were talking in the living room, on that hot summer day, we were sitting on the threshold of the fire escape in the other room where some towels, recently washed, were hung out to dry. There were no washing machines in people's homes. And certainly, no dryers. There wasn't even a clothes line extending out the window to some pole. People hung small amounts of laundry on a rope tied from one end of the fire escape to the other. It was temporary and the towels, rung out by Julia's mother with a not very strong pair of hands, were still dripping, or very close to that. For some reason both of us chose a towel and began to suck the moisture out of the edges of the towel. We were afraid of being caught by our mothers, but only slightly. Worse went to worse, the towels would be rinsed out again and no harm done. But we were more ashamed of being such babies—sucking away at the possibly still-a-little-soapy towels. We were three years old at the time. We were able to walk, and talk, and to realize that this was planned parental playtime. But neither one of us knew how to play. So, we giggled a little in between our interactions with our individual towels. The time passed.

Later when Julia's parents were the first among us to get a small television, we would all come over, sometimes on Sunday afternoon, for an hour or so and watch what was on television. But that was quite a bit later, perhaps four or five years later. No towel sucking then.

When we moved away from that neighborhood, about a mile away, that's only about twenty city blocks away, it was light years away for our families. The only connection we retained was that both of us girls did go to Hungarian dancing classes for children. But Julia was not at all interested in dancing and moved like a stick figure, frozen by the thought of making a mistake. Her body didn't bend in the middle, her knees didn't bend, and neither did her ankles. So, although she was a pretty little girl with blonde curls and well-carved features, as well as a flawless complexion, no one paid her any attention in the class. On the other hand, I was happy dancing. My body and mind, and even my soul, moved to the rhythm of the music comfortably, joyously. I never complained that it was too much work or too hard. I

THE BLOCK

never asked to rest. And the other girls, who felt about moving the way I did, wanted to dance with me, just as I wanted to dance with them.

I rarely danced with Julia.

She dropped out of dance class when her little brother was born. That is, she dropped out of Hungarian dance class. This was after the war. Social contact among Hungarians was now no longer seen as a threat to the security of . . . I'm not sure what. I suppose the city, or the nation, or the world? But Julia did join the ballet class because her parents thought it would give her grace of movement, in which she continued to need improvement, just to move like a girl.

I have no idea of her interests at school. As far as I know, she became a nurse in later life. That is, when she was in her twenties. By that time, we'd lost touch. Even though she herself was not apparently important in my life, she was a catalyst for an important step in my life. Because, as I mentioned a little while ago, she was having a Sweet Sixteen party, her birthday party, and her parents had made it a big event, a catered-hired-hall event, although on a working-class scale. And, I was invited to her party.

I may have known that she had a cousin, or not. I certainly had never seen him or met him or knew anything about his family or life. Julia's father and her cousin's father were not on speaking terms, so their families avoided each other. But apparently, they felt that, as teenagers, we should all be included in celebrating this big event for Julia.

As was the case with all my clothes, my mother made me a new dress for the party. While I had some say in the choice of fabric and style, I had nothing to do with making the dress. The fabric was a red pique, a rather heavy cotton fabric and stiff. The dress had a square neckline and, of course, had sleeves, short sleeves, but sleeves to hide my pimples. The red was very bright and pure. The dress fit snugly to my waist, which was small, and then flared out with the dirndl skirt, nicely sculpted so that it didn't look bulky, but only looked full. It was the style then to have dresses extend below the knee, and actually somewhat down the calf, in length. My long wavy brown hair covered my neck and part of my face. My eyes were so dark a brown that they looked almost black. My coloring went well with the dress.

Needless to say, or maybe not, I was the only one there with a bright red dress on. When I walked into

THE BLOCK

the basement hall, where the party was being held, I was noticed. I haven't the foggiest idea what people were noticing, but they looked.

One person who looked was Julia's cousin whose name was Alex, as he introduced himself. The Hungarian form of his name—what his parents, and I think his relatives, called him—was Sandor.

I couldn't help noticing him, either. First of all, he was the tallest person, by far, in the room. And because he was in military uniform, an Air Force uniform, and was the only person in the room dressed that way. I must admit, I also noticed that he was handsome, blonde with very even features and a gentle, naïve expression on his face.

I don't remember what we talked about. All I know is that he walked me home. The party was on Eighty-Second Street and I lived on Eightieth Street. I found out that he lived on Eighty-Ninth Street, which was akin to living in Alaska in terms of the communication that I would likely ever have had with him. It was completely understandable that I had never met him before. Or even seen him before, for that matter.

We probably talked about what he was doing in his life, as a student in a community college and his being in the Air Force Reserve. There was no way that I was going to invite him up to my home. My family didn't easily have guests upstairs.

Since he and I wanted to talk a little more, we walked over to the trusty stoop, where so much of my life had been spent. Soon I was leaning against the pillar on the right railing of the stoop.

And he was getting closer to me. At some point his knee rested on the step in front of us and came close to my body. Although he didn't kiss me at that time, there was a connection between our bodies. That was a new experience for me. And later, I found out, for him as well.

He was eighteen years old. And, like his cousin, I was sixteen.

Somehow, we agreed to meet in two weeks, since he had weekend military service the following weekend. After that, things just developed till he met my family. And I met his. We became a regular pinochle-foursome in my house. His Hungarian was limited and mine was sufficient with his parents.

THE BLOCK

Sometimes awkwardly, we all communicated with each other to the extent that that was possible, based on our differing family interests and personalities. Our parents only formally interacted with each other.

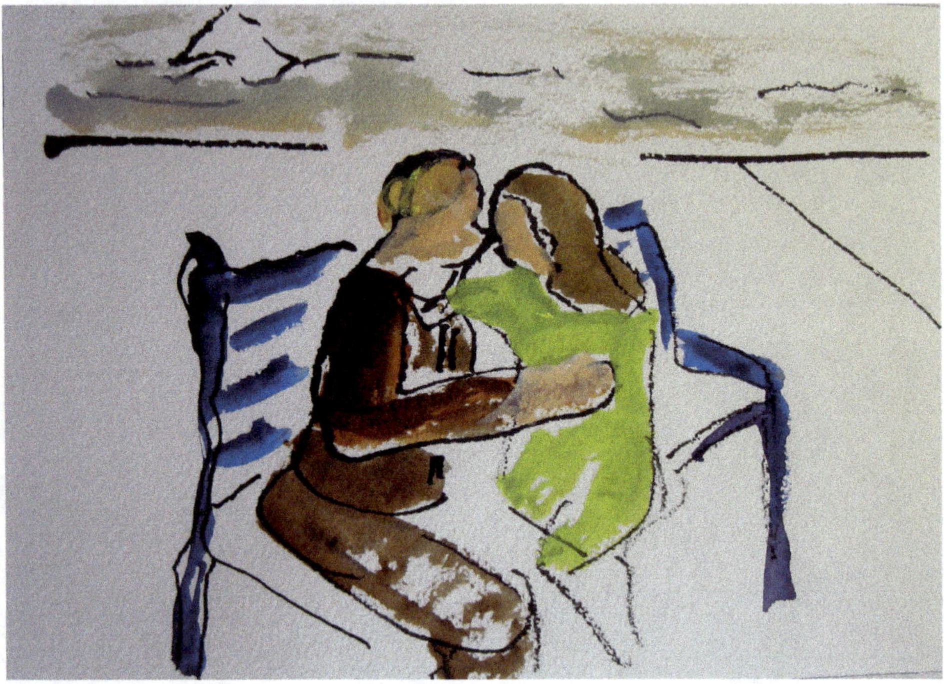

5. Beside the River

The third time we got together, Alex and I took a walk. Block to block, house to house, the neighborhood changed. After the row of tenement houses, there was a candy store, a bike shop, and the store of the ice and coal man. Coal for the belly stoves and ice for the ice-boxes for families that did not have refrigerators yet. As we walked farther down towards the river, the neighborhood got even poorer. And it was dark. The back-end of the church, which fronted on a main crossing a block away, was unlit, unprotected, and uncomfortable to walk past.

But I didn't like going to that church from the front either. Inside it was cold, marble, huge and often

THE BLOCK

empty, because it was much too large for the community it was serving. All the priests were Irish in the church and most of the people who lived in the block behind it were Irish, too, and had many children. Consequently, even though their parents had the same amount of money coming in every week as the families in the previous block, that money had to be spread not just three ways or four ways, but eight or ten ways, as the families grew larger.

Going farther towards the river there were outdoor parking lots, indoor parking lots, mechanic shops, and not far from the river, there was a live poultry market.

Every week I visited that market with my mother and bought the chicken for the week. Rarely, perhaps twice a year, she bought a duck. I couldn't stand by while she picked the duck, because I thought they were so beautiful. The thought that we would be the cause of its death was more than I could handle. And once every year, at Christmastime, a goose.

My mother carefully examined the bird before buying it. She looked at its feet, felt the flesh on its breast bone, and examined its eyes. Once selected, the bird was fresh killed toward the back of the store by slitting its neck. Then it was allowed to hang by its feet until the blood had drained from the animal, from where its throat had been cut. The bird was next gutted, washed, and placed on a rotating-prickly-churning cylinder that removed most of the feathers, without scarring the skin. At the customer's request, the feet were removed and placed alongside the liver, gizzard and heart to be packed with the chicken itself. Generally, the head was removed and was not taken home by the customer. But the neck definitely was brought back, because it was excellent for chicken stock.

Crossing the large Avenue, just before the Riverwalk entrance, was like entering a new and very different world of tall, modern apartment buildings with doormen and maintenance people, with housekeepers, with take-in food and take-out laundry. Within three blocks, Alex and I had traveled from the working class, to the lower class, to the block with establishments like garages and poultry markets. Only to wind up smack in the middle of the narrow island of the middle class that bordered one end of the island and the river.

Walking up the steps at the end of the street bordering the side entrances of these middle-class,

THE BLOCK

actually upper-middle-class houses, we were led directly to the walk along the river. There were nine steps. It was dark and necessary to be careful because no one knew who was doing what underneath the steps. Sleeping, urinating strangers. Or some person planning harmful behavior, even robbery.

But Alex and I didn't have anything much to steal. A few dollars, if that much. He had a stainless-steel watch, and I had a tiny gold chain around my neck, unadorned. Alone, I would have been frightened, but with him, I was not. It just felt peaceful that we were finally away from observing parents and neighbors and friends.

At the top, we leaned on the curved metal railing and watched the water move. Enjoyed the lights flashing on it. Sometimes a small tugboat would pass by. Sometimes even a barge. It was silent, even when a boat went by. And the silence, too, was a balm to our agitated city experience.

The breeze always picked up near the river. On this night, in a pleasant way, it took any discomfort of the summer heat away and cleansed each of us, and both of us together. We sat down on one of the metal benches, not particularly comfortable. But it seemed more than adequate, even wonderful to be there.

As the breeze got stronger, Alex put his arm around me, and I snuggled in against the folds of his shirt. Although we had hugged before on the stoop the first night we met, this was the first real contact that we made. The kids used to say, by not leaving room for the Holy Ghost. We moved from his having one arm around me, to his other arm being around my waist. As we slowly, but clearly, moved closer, a kiss was as natural as breathing. After a rest and another kiss, we had gradually moved closer, not just physically, but emotionally as well. His hand gently approached my clothed breast. I didn't know it at the time, but this was a first for him.

Since the only experiences I had had with kissing were the spin the bottle or flashlight games played in groups, this was new for me. And soon I found out it was new for him, too. He said, "I didn't know I could feel this way. I thought there was something wrong with me because I couldn't respond the way that I heard the other boys and young men responding. And now I know that I can. It's incredible. Thank you for showing me that I'm okay."

THE BLOCK

"I didn't do it for that. I kissed you because I wanted to. I didn't know I had this much feeling in me either."

Those moments, which constituted nothing more than kissing, were to determine not just the course of the next eight years of our lives, but our entire future. It was the beginning of being free from those parental ties that bind, which everyone knows about and few are able to leave behind them. As we walked slowly, very slowly, toward my parents' house, we were now not just walking side-by-side, but walking holding hands, and not speaking very much. As we reached the stoop, the stoop where we had talked the first night we met — the night with me in my red dress and him in his Air Force uniform — we stopped by the pillar at the bottom of the handrail. We stood still, looked at each other and kissed each other lightly, before he walked me on, one house more, to where I lived. The self-same house, the self-same steps, yet now I was alive in a new way, and a step farther toward growing up.

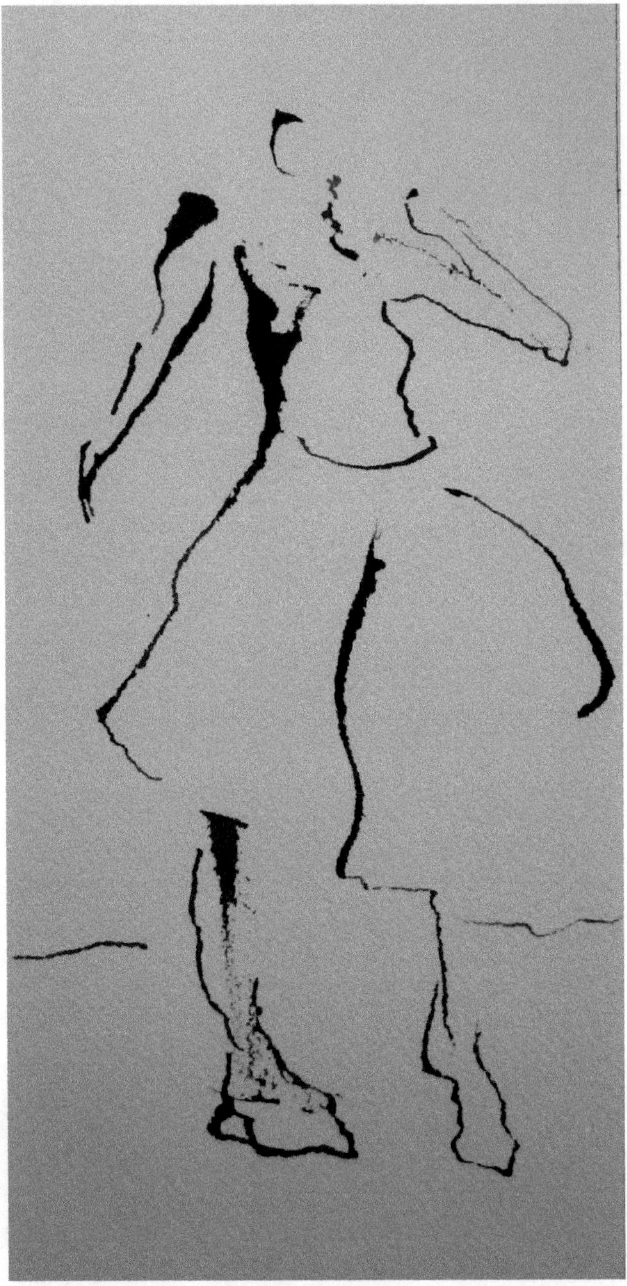

6. The Little Brown Gabardine Skirt

All that anyone could see, as she ran up the dimly lit stairs, was the sway of her brown skirt all rumpled and wet down the front. Her pale little knees, trembling with each step, she silently sobbed as she climbed. Soon her raised and outstretched arms were visible as she approached the top of the stairs and another brown gabardine skirt, just like hers. She bumped into the girl wearing it and pushed her aside to continue running, it's not clear where. It was as if she would keep running forever, away from where she'd been and towards she knew not what.

THE BLOCK

PART ONE

Where to start? I mean there are two places I could start my story. I could ask you, and with sincerity, how would you feel if your father, your mother's and your only source of stability and support, had collapsed on the job, on the train from Philadelphia back home to New York? He did. And what are we supposed to do? That would be one start.

Another way would be to say that I'm the only redhead on the block. It's just me, and Rita Hayworth, that people talk about because, like her, I'm special. It's not just that I'm a redhead, a natural redhead. No. I'm clever and the few freckles on my clear complexion make me so cute that everyone smiles when they see me. I'm a ball of energy and everyone wants to be friends with me.

Like there's this girl next-door, well actually three doors away, who is always hanging around and trying to get me to be her friend. I mean, she's okay. But just okay. She doesn't play games very well, although lately it looks like she's really good at school. I say lately because before last year, when they gave these big state tests, IQ tests they called them, until then, she was caught cheating one day on a spelling test and everybody assumed that she cheated a lot and that's why she got good grades. Still, everybody on the block had to admit that she could not have cheated on the state-sponsored, universal tests. And she seems to have scored off the charts, so I guess she's smart enough. Maybe she didn't cheat all the time. But you can see how special I am, how clearly I see everything and that's why I'm the boss on the block, even over the boys, and even though I'm a girl. And that other girl . . ., she cries all the time. I hate that.

Not only do I look like Rita Hayworth, but, by the way, my name is Rosie. See what I mean? And I can dance the mambo like nobody you've ever seen, except maybe a movie star like Rita Hayworth. And I know that's true because my aunt is married to a Puerto Rican, and she dances the incredible mambo with him. What a pair. Every time she comes over, she and I dance together, and I get better and better at it.

So, you can see I'm a pretty big shot on the block, even by eight years old. And here comes the sniffling girl, from three houses down, with another friendship offering, a bribe. No, maybe she's just nice, but she

THE BLOCK

gets on my nerves. This time she's bringing a small package in her hand and, as she climbs up the single flight of marble stairs, I can see her reaching out. I know she's going to give me that package. It's usually nice, what she gives, but I always feel uncomfortable when this happens.

In fact, the present this time is a small brown skirt. Actually, there are two skirts in the bag. Identical skirts. And she has brought one for me and the other to show me that now we can dress like twins sometimes. . . Okay. The skirt is nice, and it fits, and we have no money for new clothes, with my father the way he is, in and out of the hospital. No money. "It's running out very soon," I hear my mother saying. Anyway, there is no blouse with the skirt, so I guess I'll have to use one that I already have. That's okay. I'm clever and if anyone makes me uncomfortable, seeing the two of us in the same kind of skirt, I'll think of something smart to say.

Something to make me look good and maybe even make her look just a little pathetic. I mean, I know that Rita Hayworth wasn't always nice either, and neither is my aunt or my mother. My father is nice, and look what happened to him. So, what road would you choose? I choose to be strong and live, and be the boss. Yeah, that's better. I'll wait a while to wear this skirt. I don't know, a couple of weeks. I don't want her to think that it means very much to me. If she thinks that, she will stop giving me things. And, to tell the truth, I like the things she gives me. After all her father is a tailor and her mother sews really well. And, just to remind you, we have no money now.

That's no exaggeration. Yesterday we had cupcakes, bought as day-old cupcakes from the bakery around the corner. My parents drank a cup of tea with them, and there was some milk to put in my tea. I don't really feel hungry most of the time. And I certainly get plenty of dessert. But I wouldn't mind a bologna sandwich sometimes. With lettuce and a slice of tomato, and a nice big spoonful of mayonnaise. That wouldn't be bad. Not bad at all. Today there's been nothing to eat so far, except for our cup of coffee that my mom makes every morning in the drip pot. It's not very strong, but it's hot and welcoming in the morning.

It's different when my grandmother comes over every week or so, she only lives three blocks away, but it's not easy for her to come. Well, it's not so much that it's hard for her to come over. It's that she doesn't really approve of my father, who is Irish. She's

THE BLOCK

German, and she thinks that she is superior. She knows that she is superior. She's always reminding us that she's superior, when she comes here. She can't understand why my mother married a man like this, a railroad employee, rather than a schoolteacher, a good German with a respectable job. Lower-class choice, definitely. Puzzling though . . . Everyone loved him. He had a way of making people laugh and feel happy that they had seen him. I bet that's why my mom married him. What a relief he must've been from my grandmother's humorless, harsh rigidity.

Mom had some of this rigidity, too, but she was more fragile, somehow. Maybe. Unlike my robust grandmother, Mom was so skinny. Sure, she didn't eat much, mostly because she'd gone on a starvation diet as a teenager. It was so severe that, afterwards, her stomach shrank, so she was only able to eat tiny portions at a time. Her body had become used to that scarcity. She was literally skin and bones. The grapefruit diet, I think it was, when she ate only grapefruit for a long time. The weight came off, for sure. And stayed off, for sure.

Her home was clean and neat. So was her family. She didn't care much about learning or grades at school. She enjoyed gossiping with the other women on the block, or just watching the goings-on on the street from her perch at the front room window. So, my report cards, as long as I passed, were fine with her. And Dad worked such long hours, sometimes double shift, that by the time he got home, he could only think of getting into bed fast. Next day, another long hard day of work lay ahead of him. He loved his job, in spite of how hard he had to work. Traveling, being in motion on a nice train with lots of people, different people every day, made him happy. A neat clean home was great, but, he had to say, a little empty, except when his little redhead was around and awake.

But even at home, he collapsed. Just like that. Yes. At home that night, he had another seizure, the second after his first at work, and was taken to the hospital. He spent days and days in the hospital, only to come home and still be barely able to move. Certainly unable to go to work.

His limited leave from work did last a couple months. But eventually he had to give up hoping to go back to the job he loved. They couldn't have him collapsing amidst the passengers on the train, scaring them, even being dangerous to them, while not fulfilling his duties, or the image of the railroad line.

THE BLOCK

Mom's brother was a butcher and could help him get into the union. Could he work there? He hated killing anything, and what if he collapsed? He could be a real danger to fellow workers. Then there was the question of health and hygiene where food was prepared. Out of the question.

But eating was necessary, and so was paying the rent. His unemployment benefits did run out. And he did get a bit stronger. Someone suggested he be a doorman in one of the big buildings nearby, the big luxury buildings around the nearby blocks. As a night doorman, he wouldn't have as much stress to deal with as in the daytime. And as I've said, everyone likes him, even the way he is now. The pay wasn't as good as on the railroad. He was too young to collect a pension from them.

So, in the meantime, he became a doorman. Once or twice he did have or feel a seizure coming on at night, when no one was around. But he had pills now, and he'd take one and sit for a while. Generally, it passed soon enough that he was not observed, caught, I guess.

As his daughter, for me, going to school every day was a mixed bag. On the one hand, I was glad to get out of the house. To not have to live in fear that my father, no matter what my grandmother said — my beloved father — would have another seizure that day. There was always a chance of an ambulance responding to a fall. Or even of his having the other kind of seizure, the even more dangerous one, when one of us might be slapped, accidentally, by his flailing arms and unquiet legs. I hurt inside that I never knew whether he would die when I wasn't there. Then I would never see him again. So, it wasn't so much whether I liked school or didn't like school — school just didn't matter that much. He did. My dinner did. Being safe did.

Lately, probably because I was nervous so much of the time, I drank a lot of water to fill me up when I felt hungry. I peed a lot. Not so much "a lot" but often. I usually went to school. And I usually did have to ask to go to the girls room to pee. The teacher and the other kids were getting used to this pattern of my having to raise my hand and go down two flights of stairs to the bathroom and come back. I had learned the way, as you can see. And I went by myself. After school, if everything had been pretty quiet that day, I'd go out on the street or look out the window to hear and see whether the kids were out and talking. Sometimes they called up to my window to ask me to

THE BLOCK

come down. Our railroad flat had windows in the front, in the living room, facing the street and also at the other end of the apartment, in the bathroom, facing the back yard. In the living room, the "front room," there was a cushion on the windowsill to lean on. When I was downstairs, and my father was quiet or asleep, my mother spent a lot of time just watching the people outside that window, her elbows cushioned on the windowsill inside.

She didn't go for a walk much. She didn't really like to go out of the neighborhood. And for her, the neighborhood was only one block long, our block, plus, without crossing the street, about halfway around to each of the Avenues. That was true before my father was sick. That had been true for as long as I can remember. She was scared. Her world consisted in her meticulously clean apartment, in spite of their only source of heat being a coal stove, a belly stove, in the kitchen. A bucket of coal was delivered from down the block twice a week. The tub was in the kitchen, too — the bathtub. Now you know how come I never went to my grandmother's house, though her apartment only three blocks away. My mother didn't travel at all, and I couldn't travel alone, yet.

Other people, other women on the block, did leave the block. Some every day. That included the mother of the pesky girl. The one whose mother made the skirt for me. She was away all the time. My mother and she said, "Hello" and exchanged a couple words, if they met, but they were not friends. I'm not sure either one of them knew how to make a friend with anybody. My mother's life was too confined. Her mother was always on the run. Was all this because of the war? People being so scared?

I wasn't scared. I liked to go places when I could. But if I couldn't go places, as you already know, I like to be the boss, at least on the block.

PART TWO

There are two sides to every story. At least. I have no idea . . . That's not true. I do know why she doesn't like me. No matter how I try to show her I like her. I don't think she sees me as an equal. No matter how good my grades are. Or how people praise me and give me special jobs to do at school, because the curriculum is too simple for me.

THE BLOCK

We were "best friends" who didn't really know each other. I expect it's a lot to expect that two children, at nine years old, would know this is the basis for friendship. Or even if they did know it, I'm not sure they knew how to do it. Every time I tried to talk with her, she'd change the subject or propose any game she was sure to win.

Everybody, including me, was fascinated by her red hair and her energy. I had energy when I was dancing, but when it came to playing hop-scotch or hit-the-penny ball, or any other game for that matter, I just couldn't do it. I invariably lost. She would make fun of me. I would try to fight back unsuccessfully with words. Words had no effect on her. When once or twice I tried to slap her, I couldn't connect the slap. And I wound up humiliated, as well as losing. And in tears. Rosie yelled, "Crybaby. You're nothing but a crybaby." She'd keep saying it until I ran away, crying all the way home. And crying when I got there, too. I seemed to have an unlimited quantity of tears in me and seemed unable to think of any other way of handling her and those situations. Being smart on IQ tests didn't help one bit. And, to top it all, when I got home, there was usually nobody there.

Stefan Draughon

I hoped we could be "sisters." I so wanted someone, a sister or a brother, my own size at home. After all, sisters fight with each other sometimes, but it doesn't break up the relationship. It's expected. Sibling rivalry. But girlfriends, especially nine-year-old dreamers, expect to get along, to be on the same side and be pals. Kids against adults, or whatever. But allies on the same side.

I felt alone and lonely no matter what I did. I succeeded at doing things, but not in being friends. At least, not girlfriends. Some of the boys talked to me. They didn't interrupt a beginning conversation with suggestions to play a game. But they rarely felt comfortable sitting down with any girl for any reason. They were also nine years old.

The day I rang Rosie's bell, with the skirt in my hand, I thought she might like to be twins — to dress alike sometimes. I thought she would like my mother's sewing and be grateful. But she wasn't. By the time I got upstairs and stepped into her apartment, I saw she wasn't pleased. I looked to her mother for support and then said stupid things. Like: "I hope you like the skirt." I don't remember her response. So, I upped the ante and said my parents would fix things for them, if they needed a tailor. And

THE BLOCK

that didn't work either. Rosie and her mother just stood there trying to figure out what I was about. Of course, I began to cry, ran out the door and down the stairs, home. A joke on me. A home that never felt like home, that I couldn't wait to leave. Being a kid, for me, was the pits. I never did figure out what praise of childhood was all about. I saw it as a disease I needed to out-grow, as quickly as possible.

However, when I got home, my parents asked about their reaction to the skirt. I couldn't bring myself to say that there was no response at all. Instead, I lied. I said that they had asked if my parents could shorten Rosie's mother's winter coat. My parents resented their ungrateful forwardness and were irritated at the lack of appreciation of their work. Of all the unmitigated gall on their part, to make such a request. I then cried longer and harder and finally wound up confessing that I had lied to my parents. That the repair of the coat was my idea, not theirs. They had simply said nothing.

Although I was accustomed to being reprimanded by my mother for being fresh, this time both parents agreed that lying, especially to them, was strictly out of the question. Off-limits. They were angry with me.

And sorry they had ever agreed make the skirt, the second brown gabardine skirt, at all.

So you can see that, in addition to doing well at school, I had great skill in messing up my relationships, all around. I understood, even then, that I was in search of love. But how? What could I do? I had no idea then that love is a grace and comes only when freely given by another person. There's nothing I could have done. No. Yet everything, too. Choosing to be with people who generally liked me from the start, for example. Then letting them freely decide on the next step one way or the other. I already knew how to mess it up by pushing my neediness at them, clinging, and trying to "buy" their love.

When they calmed down, they asked me, upfront, why I continued to pursue this child's attention, when she clearly was not interested in me. I had no answer then. But I knew that I would not lie to my parents ever again.

As it is with kids, or with any relatively uncommitted relationship, Rosie and I patched things together a little. We did wear our brown skirts one day. This day. The day when everything changed.

PART THREE

Yes, the two girls patched it up with each other at least enough so that they each wore their brown skirts on the same day. But, unlike what they had expected, nobody really noticed. Nobody said anything at all. Class was just as it usually was. Every child in a different place in mind and in heart.

The redhead especially needed to go to the bathroom that day. Maybe she was nervous, or just needed to get out of confined space of the classroom with the confining presence of Mrs. Morgan. This teacher didn't hurt these girls, or any children in the class, for that matter. But her attitude was detached and uncaring. In both her dress and demeanor, she was sharp and gray — not alive for the kids. She behaved as if something was bothering her, something that had nothing to do with her job, yet nevertheless impacted on her job and her way of being with her students.

So when a hand was raised towards the back of the class and the redhead had to "be excused" again, the teacher expressed no noticeable affect. She made some kind of rational decision, it seemed, that it was better to let her go to the bathroom than run the risk of having a mess to clean up in the classroom, especially since they were just about to have a projector brought in so that the class could see a movie. The film was "David Copperfield" and the super-intelligent girl, who would miss the least by being out of the classroom for a while, was sent to pick up the machine.

Once she brought the projector back, it was clear that the teacher had forgotten to ask her to get the film. But before she went on this second errand, Mrs. Morgan also wrote a note for her to take to the Librarian on her way to the library for the film. The girl was trustworthy about not snooping at her notes. Mrs. Morgan felt so uncomfortable dealing with the problem she was having at home that kept buzzing around in her head, that she needed to talk to someone. It simply would not abandon her consciousness. Maybe if the Librarian and she talked at lunch time. Maybe then she could feel better in the afternoon.

Both girls were out of the classroom at the same time. One on an errand for the teacher, and the other on a call of nature. The librarian read the note and wrote a reply. She also took longer to find the film than usual. So, the child had to wait to go back to class.

The library was two flights upstairs from the classroom. As the child was returning to the classroom with the film, another child, coming from below, bumped into her sharply. All they could both see at that moment were the two identical, brown gabardine skirts. There were no words, just a sharp bump. This time the tears rolled down the cheeks of the eyes-averted-redheaded child whose skirt was visibly soiled.

PART FOUR

The Girls' bathroom was moderately large, with seven stalls, big enough for sixth graders, not just kindergarten kids. The light was always left on, and the ceramic-tile floor sparkled, having recently been cleaned by the janitor. Rosie walked in, barely able to contain her bladder. Before reaching the first stall, she was able to lift her skirt and get her panties down. She got there in time. Quickly enough that she didn't get wet. It was bad enough to have to keep popping out of the classroom, but to go back there wet, was even worse.

She was in such a hurry that she forgot to lock the bathroom door before she started to pee. When she turned around, getting dressed, she thought she heard something. She'd been in here many times before and never had heard anything. Maybe it was the janitor just finishing up late. She knew him. And he always made her laugh, just like her father did. She didn't know if he was Irish or not. He certainly was "Honorary Irish."

But she remembered that he always had his bucket and mop with him. They rattled and banged on the floor. That's not what she'd heard. Now she heard no such sound. Except, there was a sound.

She carefully prepared herself to run out, and upstairs to her classroom. But, as she opened the door, she did see someone there. A man. A strange, middle-aged man. Kind of puffy in the face. All red in the face, too. On seeing each other, they both stood still, as she fixed to run away. This was no friendly and kind janitor. Instead of saying anything, the stranger reached out, as if noticing her red hair, staring at it oddly, longingly, weirdly. That whole

THE BLOCK

period of time seem to be in slow-motion, although it was not.

After touching her hair and her dress, he moved in closer, touching her all over. Then closer still, until she was pushed back into the stall she had just left, being pressed against the toilet seat. Usually she was loud and talked easily. Now she was in shocked-silence. Wide-eyed, disbelieving, confused, she kicked him in the leg. The shin was all she could reach.

But the kick was impotent although he, it became increasingly clear, was not. With all of his pushing, he simultaneously opened the zipper on his pants, and slowly brought out his penis, getting larger as it emerged from the zipper. He was not pleased with himself and his growing erection. Not happy at all. Only crazed and wild. She'd never seen anything like this before. It was like a big stick coming at her, like a bald, fetal animal, all reddish-purple and angry. It became his face, this terrifying ugly face with no hint of kindness in it. Soon it was resting, not really resting but gyrating on her clothes, her skirt, her panties, her legs. She thought it would never stop. She thought It —no He— was killing her. As a good Irish child, she began to pray "Hail Mary full of grace..."

But it did stop. And she was all wet. She thought she'd peed on herself. But the wet was sticky. She'd never peed like that. Distracted by whether she had wet herself or not, she stopped looking at him or at that terrifying fetus thing. And when she did look up, there was no one there. Somehow, silently and quickly, he had left. She unthawed enough to slowly peer out and around the stall wall and saw nothing. No footprints, no fetus, no man, nothing but the row of empty sinks leading to the door of the bathroom.

She stopped and stood still for a moment to look down at her body, at her skirt, at her legs. She didn't bother to try to wipe herself off. She didn't do anything, except run. Run up the stairs. Run one flight and another till she was on the third floor, the classroom floor. Her arms were extended, and now, she was crying, really silently sobbing, as she bumped into the girl wearing a brown gabardine skirt. The one just like hers. Pushing her aside, Rosie searched and searched for something that was not made out of brown fabric and was taller than herself. Was there something like that out there?

THE BLOCK

PART FIVE

For weeks, everyone in the neighborhood could talk of nothing else. "The child, poor child, what a terrible thing to happen in school." It had never happened before in that neighborhood. What could be done about it? Where would the child go now? She couldn't go back to school. She was traumatized. How would the other children understand what had happened? They wouldn't. They were too young. Yes. The best thing was for her to go to Florida, for a visit. Really, she could stay with her aunt out there for a while.

The police had no clues. There'd been no previous incidents in the neighborhood. Nobody was suspect. And this was 1949, when everybody knew each other on the block.

There was this weird man living far down the block with his mother. But he was harmless and seemed terrified of everyone rather than any threat to anyone. In any case, no one had seen him anywhere near the school, let alone in it, either that day or any other day. No. He didn't do it. Besides the important thing was the child, the sparklingly clever, redheaded child who had been terrified and molested.

Neighbors now said, "That thing about the skirts. That was strange." And her pushing the other girl away like that, almost slamming her into the wall, uncaringly. Yeah. The neighbors said this, but really no one cared about the pushed child. Her life might have been affected by all this, too.

PART SIX

Six months later both girls were living in their homes, just as they had before the school "molestation," everyone said, avoiding the word "rape."

A few things had changed. Some rather large. The redheaded girl no longer went to the same school, but went instead to the Catholic school down the block. At the school where the incident had occurred, children were no longer allowed to leave the classroom to go to the bathroom by themselves. Instead two children were sent down together each time. The crime continued to be not only unsolved,

THE BLOCK

but the police were still clueless as to who had done this, and how it could have occurred.

These were surface changes. On a deeper level the friendship between the two girls was affected. It was as if the skirt, the brown gabardine skirt, once a gift, had magically become tainted and became a symbolic precipitating-cause of the redhead's having been violated.

Later, each child went to a different school after the sixth grade. The redhead went to secretarial school and started working as soon as she could get working papers. She actually became more cheerful and much less bossy. A nicer person. Maybe she wasn't as clever, or maybe she was learning about what she really needed in her life.

On the surface, it was reasonable to think that the redhead would have been most deeply affected and hurt by the crime inflicted on her. In fact, at eighteen, she married the waiter she met by yelling across her backyard window down to the outdoor restaurant garden on the other side of the backyard, thereby forming a relationship with the young waiter which led to a lifelong marriage including three children, all healthy.

The other child went to school outside the neighborhood which was for gifted girls, and found others like herself. The "Crybaby" never could give up feeling the pain of what it happened to her friend. And feeling somehow responsible for it. Throughout her life, she felt the intensity of her relationships, not only with this girl, this redheaded girl, but with everyone. Somehow what happened that day at school to Rosie, and, in popular opinion, had not happened to her, nevertheless stuck on her like double-sticky scotch tape that it took decades to pull away from her body and her mind.

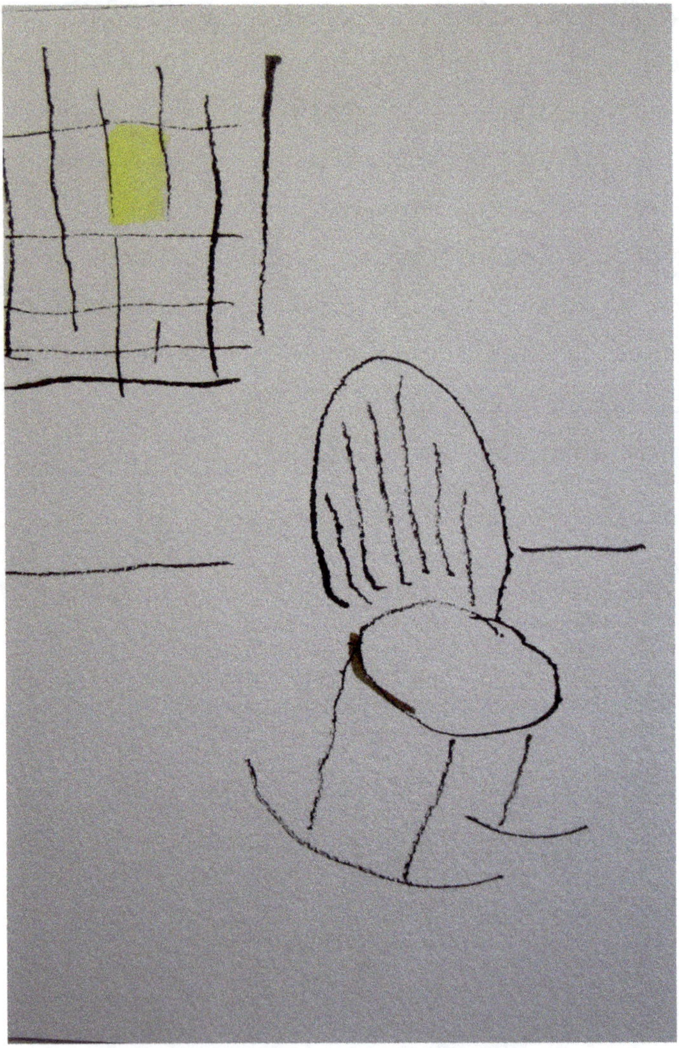

7. Cathy in D.C.

Penn Station was unusually busy the day I was to catch the train to Washington, D.C. I'd been there many times with my parents, but this was the first time I was traveling from New York alone on the train. At thirteen years old, I looked older than my age, maybe nineteen or even twenty-five, so I didn't stand out too much among the other travelers. I was a little scared. But mostly it was exciting to be traveling by myself to see my aunt, who was wonderful to be with. Plus, her first baby had just been born a few months before. A double treat.

Actually, a triple treat. Being on my own and away from my parents. I couldn't wait to be fully grown up,

THE BLOCK

separate and free. I'd gone with them New York to Chicago a couple times, and even to Florida once. All overnight trips. Train travel was fun. My parents sat together, so I could sit alone and enjoy looking out the window for hours at a time, even talking to the person next to me, or walking on the jiggly surface of the moving train to the bathroom or the café car. Mostly I had the luxury to sit and read for long periods of time without someone telling me there was something else I was supposed to do. Or at home, having to read with the television blasting sports or news at the other end of the small room. Three people living in a one-bedroom apartment, half tailoring shop, was a lot.

Being at the train station early, a life-long travel habit, I was towards the front on line for the train and felt quite grown-up handing my ticket to the agent and following the group down the steps to the train. And then to my seat. At that time, as now, I preferred an aisle seat in the middle of the car with a good view outside the windows on both sides of the car and with a working overhead reading light, should the car lights dim. Then I could get up and walk around whenever I liked and not have to worry about the sun shining on me, and my book, as it came up from the East. I guarded my one piece of luggage and, of course, the shopping bag with my books and the gifts for Cathy and the baby. I travelled light even though I was to stay with her for the whole summer. To keep her company? To keep me off the city streets by myself once school was out? Or for my parents to be rid of me for a while?

Cathy was alone with her baby and having trouble adjusting to the recent big changes in her life. This was her first child. She had had no experience with little kids, since she was the youngest of seven children, the "baby" herself. And her husband was away just as she was getting accustomed to the big change that her first child had brought into her life.

It would've been easier for her, if her husband could have been able to be there with her, but he was in Japan with missions to Korea during the Korean War. He had never seen his new baby and would not see her until she was three years old. When he did come home, the child didn't relate to him at all for quite a while. It took even longer for her to see him as her father. Meantime, Washington was a good place for Cathy to live. She had lived there before and knew the area. Military facilities, including the hospital where she'd given birth, were close by. She lived neither right in the middle of the city, nor too far out.

THE BLOCK

These changes in Cathy's life meant she needed a car, and she'd just gotten her driver's license the day before I arrived. Bravely, she chose to pick me up at the train station. That was both reassuring to the child in me, but also a little awkward. I was only the second person she had ever driven, with no other driver in the car. She was confident driving alone, but having a passenger was another matter. Fortunately for her, and for me, I loved and trusted her. That, combined with the fact that I wasn't a backseat driver, and that we could talk about all this, had a good result. We arrived safely and continued to drive together over the months I was there.

In her small apartment, I saw a tiny windowless kitchen. It was more like a Manhattan apartment kitchen than one that I would've expected in this relatively smaller city. There was a blue pullout couch for me to sleep on, and her double bed, with a single pillow, one side left un-slept on. And for the baby, she had a hand-carved cradle that had been Cathy's, when she herself was born. The piece of furniture I loved best was her rocker for nursing the child. This armless, small-scale rocker was the fulfillment of her fantasy of being a mother. She would be comfortable nursing in the chair without arms. She could hold the baby in different positions while nursing comfortably.

During the day we mostly talked and played with the baby. But I need to tell you upfront that Cathy was, until her death, the only person I knew who giggled with me. Everybody else was above it all, and was incapable of giggling with anybody, not just with me. But even when Cathy was ninety years old, shortly before she died, when we were in the now grown "baby's" car and "baby" was driving, Cathy and I were sitting, huddled next to each other in the backseat. I don't know, but she said something or I said something, and we started giggling. And couldn't stop. What is it about giggling that makes it so rare in adults? Even in children, sometimes? Does being grown-up mean being a non-giggler? You think? Boy, do I miss her and it deeply.

***

As Cathy became comfortable taking the baby out more often, and the baby nursed a little less frequently, and more on schedule, all of us went for walks. At first rather short ones and then increasingly longer. Finally, we walked toward the large building that was far off, but visible from Cathy's window, only because all the other buildings in between it and us, were then two-story row-houses. Looked like Queens does to me today.

THE BLOCK

The building was not simply far. But once we reached it, we had to either turn around and go back, or go in a different direction. Or choose to walk around it. Since it was several blocks long in each direction and heavily fenced in, what should we do that day?

For some unspecifiable reason the place seemed creepy to me. After all, it was just an ordinary brick building, neither particularly attractive nor unattractive. But I felt there was a grayness about it, as though, if I walked halfway around, I might come to harm and possibly never come back. I knew this was a silly thought, but that didn't preclude my feeling quite uncomfortable in its perimeter. How strange.

I don't know why, or how, the subject came up. Cathy was not a reader. Maybe because her husband was attached to the military, she pointed out that Ezra Pound was in that hospital right then. Since I was already interested in literature, even at that young age, I was aware that he was a famous poet. But was he crazy? Why would he be in an insane asylum? I knew nothing yet about his history before and during the war—the Second World War—but I had heard something unnerving about him and his behavior, along with his fame as a writer, particularly of poetry.

Yes, probably Cathy's husband had talked with her about Pound. He was a reader. So, about half way around St. Elizabeth's, she pointed at the building and started counting the floors and then the windows on that floor. Not like her, I thought. She counted to the exact place where Pound was being held.

I froze. To think that there was a person behind that window and that he couldn't be far away from it, possibly even looking out at us. He was so close to us somehow. She explained what she had learned. He was able to work there. She believed that nobody knew what to do with him after his treasonous comments before and during the war. Send him to jail? After all, he was a great poet. But he was also seen as a traitor. Being in jail would probably not only prevent his continuing to work as an artist, but he might be harmed, even killed there by the other inmates. And that could cause a ruckus, even an eruption of violence in other countries, let alone in the USA.

As a child, I wasn't writing yet, except for the required "compositions" in English class. Writing

THE BLOCK

entered my life in an active sense only as an adult. But art in all its forms were already important. I was obsessed with dancing and music and art. The thought of an artist living in a mental hospital, for his own and for his country's safety, seemed painful to me. Not that I had a better solution in mind. But maybe someone would come up with one. Yes, there must be a better solution. Didn't we have freedom of speech in this country? Where is the line in wartime? Boy, I was sure I didn't know.

At thirteen, I had no idea that I would later spend almost ten years of my life on the psychology staff in places like St. Elizabeth's to support my art and explore other parts of the mind. The unconscious mind does not just operate in dreams. But in paintings and poems and songs as well. Besides, what a strange name for a mental hospital, a saint's name. I wondered if it was named after the same St. Elizabeth as the church I attended, and was devoted to, in New York.

As we walked back to Cathy's home, and for years to come—even till today—I saw, in my mind's eye, a man quartered among the insane. Was he that much different from the people that surrounded him during the war? Yes, he was alien and said traitorous things.

But if there had not been a war, or before the war, how would and did people see him and react to him then? After all, in history other artists were unpleasant as people, at least according to reputation. Artists like Beethoven or Cezanne. True, they were not speaking out in treasonous words, but still, where did they belong? In mental hospitals? Van Gogh was hospitalized in an asylum, but they let him out. Then he died, killed himself. Was that convenient, his dying? Otherwise what would have become of him?

When we reached the door to Cathy's home, I looked at the tiny child, still in the carriage, and realized there was no way to predict what her life would be like. I imagined Ezra Pound's mother looking at her baby and being unable to see his future.

I was not like the other kids in school or on the block. True, nobody was afraid of me. And I didn't act strangely in any way. Yet, as I look back, I was different from the other kids. They were right about that. I was an artist and thought differently from them at that time, and continued to do so all my life. How can the life of an artist be wonderful and exciting and, at the same time, be so separating from others, and lonely?

THE BLOCK

After Cathy, who was holding the baby, and I climbed the stairs and got to her apartment, we made dinner. What was on my mind was apparently not the same as what was on her mind. She realized that I had only brought dresses and skirts with me. She asked if I had any slacks. I said, "No." The only pants I ever wore were as costumes in local dramatic productions, where I had played a male role once or twice because there weren't enough boys in the dance troupe. She went to her small closet and took out an old pair of jeans and a well-worn T-shirt and gave them to me saying, "You don't have any play clothes. Use these while you're here and take them back with you when you go."

She was right. I never had had any play clothes before in my life. Over the years that followed, this first pair of jeans and the T-shirt, these play clothes, morphed into painting clothes. Her play clothes became mine, and they stayed with me. They became the center of the rest of my life.

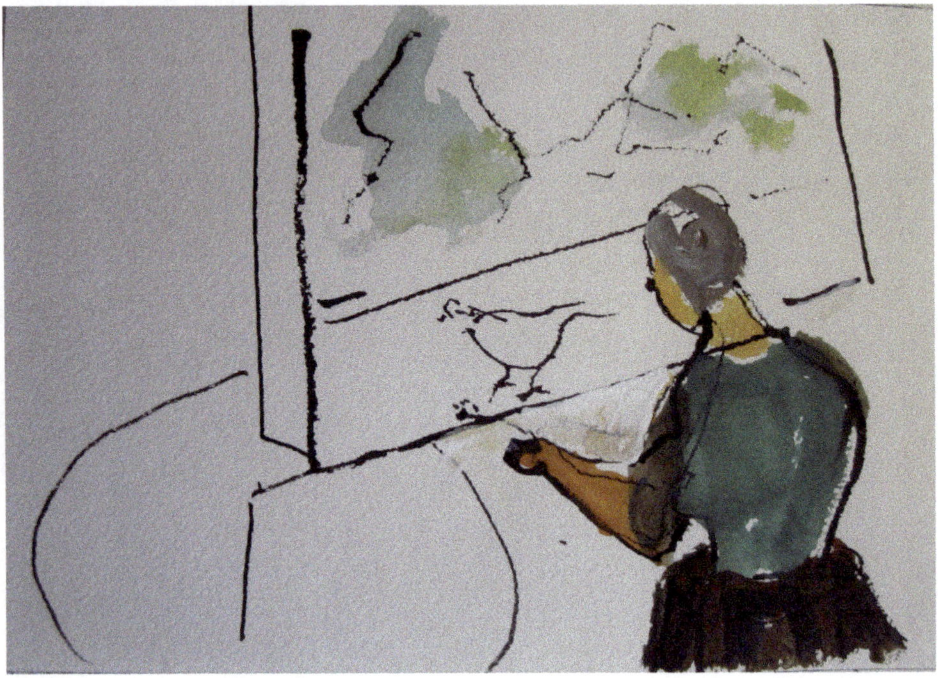

8. Mrs. Mann

When the beautiful young girl married her tall handsome man, little did she think that she would be leaving the dirt paths of central Eastern Europe. The mountains in the far distance were her friends. She had need of friends as a child. Not only did she have no siblings, but her parents worked in the wheat fields all day and were gone from home then. They were also gone from her emotionally in the early evening, when they came back exhausted from fieldwork. From the time she was tiny, she had learned to talk to the mountains. To talk to anything that stayed still long enough for her to finish her thought and offer some sense of having heard her. By the time she was four, she could feed their few

THE BLOCK

chickens. But talking to them was virtually impossible. They were squawking all the time, except when they were sleeping. Not very good company in either case. And the rooster never stayed still. He was racing around the small yard trying to find—she never found out what—but continuing to do so as if someday somewhere, on that small patch of land, he would find it. Still she tried to form relationships with them. Tried hard. But there was no good-friendship chemistry between them.

By the age of six she was able to go with other children from distant homes to help gather the wheat grains that had fallen during harvesting. In her little apron, with its large flap of an envelope in front, she carefully placed each single fallen wheat berry or stalk. On a good day, it took her all day to fill her little apron pocket. Yet she did it with pleasure, because in the distance, she could then see her parents harvesting the grain, working with the other children's parents.

She'd only begun to make the connection between the wheat berries and the bread that they ate three times a day, if they were lucky. She somehow understood that her gathering, and her parents harvesting, had something to do with her not going hungry each day. Everyone in her country had bread with every meal. And the joke — the joke that she learned much later — was that Hungarians ate bread with their bread. When she'd heard it as a child, she couldn't figure out what they were talking about. Later, it made her smile as she ate her bread with her bread.

When these families were not harvesting the wheat crop, they were tilling the soil or doing something else on the manor, directed by the officials working for the Baron. As an infant, she had only seen the Baron once, so people said. Of course, she had absolutely no recollection of having been in the same space as him. The story went that she was such a beautiful baby that he actually asked to hold her for a moment. This action became legendary throughout his manor. She was his favorite peasant child.

But this is no romance, at least not in the Hollywood sense. Although romance did come a little later, when she was fourteen and met the young man who was to be her husband the following year. They both had first names which, by the time I met them and they were in their seventies, I'm not sure that anyone but they remembered. To everyone in the neighborhood they were Mr. Mann and Mrs. Mann.

THE BLOCK

Customary formality in their country, even among the peasantry, persisted in their continuing to refer to themselves, and to each other in front of other people, as Mr. and Mrs. Mann.

How long it was between when they married and emigrated to the United States, as well as how this had been worked out, remained a mystery to all but the Mann's. They never talked about it. And no one would wish to intrude upon their privacy by asking them a personal question like that. Over their sixty years together, they maintained a relatively closed relationship with each other. It was close and uninterruptible by anyone else, except for short periods of time related to their performing some service for someone as superintendents of the building.

I met her when I was five years old. We had just moved into the apartment building two doors down from where they lived. When I then saw her, she was a very short, still-pretty woman dressed in what could easily have been the same children's apron in which she had gone out to gather remnants of the wheat harvest. Yes. She always wore the same clothes. Unlike what you might think, she was always extremely clean. Every night she washed out the garments that she and her husband had worn that day. And early in the morning, when she rose, she ironed them and they wore them again. Day, after day, after day. I never did find out whether they were so poor that they couldn't afford new clothes. Or was this simply the "waste not, want not" habit of the very poor who had neither hope nor ambition to be wealthy.

I spent time with her, that is, she kept an eye on me while my mother went to the doctor and my father was at work. In the summertime, after she had finished her work, she brought a chair or two outside. We would just sit there beside each other, next to her stoop. Hers was really not a stoop. It was simply a small set of stairs, about five, which led up to the main doorway of the four-story house that her husband managed. And managed very well. He had done so for the last forty-five years. He knew every inch of that building front and back. Only one side of the building was exposed to the outside, the other side was a shared wall with the adjacent building.

Since my mother was a sickly woman, and I was an only child, my relationship with Mrs. Mann went on for years. Not every day. No. But perhaps every two or three weeks, unless my mother was in the

THE BLOCK

hospital. Then Mrs. Mann and I were together during the day, for several days at a time. I always slept at home. Happy to see my father, when he got home from work, often very late. Always after seven or seven thirty in the evening. Sometimes even later. Then he would make a simple dinner for us. That situation lasted until I was about thirteen, when I began to make the dinner myself and only went to Mrs. Mann when I needed a little comforting.

At first Mrs. Mann and I just sat either outside or in her living room, a continuation of her kitchen, at her round wooden table, always covered with a clean tablecloth. But gradually she let me help her cook. I learned how she made various elaborate noodles, which were my childhood food passion, that continued through my adulthood. She knew more kinds of noodles than I had ever heard of. And believe me, I had made a study of noodles by the time I reached young adolescence.

The first ones we made were potato noodles. She wouldn't have been Hungarian if she thought there was only one kind of potato noodle. By the way, she might not even be married at all. After all, didn't people say that "No Hungarian man would marry a woman who couldn't cook well." So, there were at least two kinds of potato noodles, and possibly many more. But the one we made this first time was the raw potato noodles.

They were not eaten raw. The main ingredient in them was grated raw potato combined with raw eggs and flour, mixed to the consistency that, as a child, I described as "when you can hardly move the spoon in the dough anymore." The noodles, the potential noodles, were formed by placing a spoonful of the dough on a flat plate or a soup bowl that had a simple edge. Then pushing small amounts of the dough towards the edge of the plate and off it into a large pot of boiling water. These made tiny, but not too tiny, noodles when done properly. If not done properly, the spoons-full of dough made increasingly large dumplings that, by the way, never really cooked through. I know that they never cooked through, because a beloved aunt of mine made her noodles like those huge dumplings. Love her or not, those were inedible. Since I couldn't quite reach the big pot that Mrs. Mann was using, she put a small amount of dough on a small plate, and I scraped them, more or less successfully, into the boiling water in my smaller pot.

THE BLOCK

What did she do during the day you might ask? Clearly, she took care of the house. But whether she had any friends, when I first met her, I didn't know. Maybe I should've understood, after all, I was the new kid on the block. I didn't have any friends yet. Maybe she still felt like the new kid on the block, even after 45 years. I don't know.

Still, after I'd known her a year or so, she did make a friend. Not a friend that you might expect. Not another woman, similar in age to her, to cook with, and play cards and laugh with. No, no. Her new friend was a small, injured bird. A pigeon.

She told me that one whole day and night she had heard sounds on her windowsill, facing the back of the house. It was a broad sill and protected from the rain by an overhang to keep the sun out during the day, and the rain out so that Mrs. Mann could open and look out the window, even on rainy days. The sounds were being made by a small bird—a very young pigeon— who had apparently, in spite of every precaution, slammed into the partially opened window. The bird, a female, had injured her wing.

When it first arrived, the bird was puffed up into a ball and seemed to be crying, in its own way, from pain and fear. Mrs. Mann was sensitive to both pain and fear. She knew right away what the bird was feeling. And the bird knew that she meant it no harm. She was able to touch the small bird and see that the wing was broken. She put a tiny splint on the wing and brought the bird just inside the window sill, on the side of the sill extending into the apartment, so that it could be protected from not only the elements but also from small hawks and other birds of prey that would've been delighted to have this morsel for dinner.

Accustomed to being on the sill while healing, the bird soon became comfortable in all of the house and was a household member during the day. But once healed, the bird left at night to go, nobody knew where. Then the bird returned early next morning, resting and munching some food that had been left out for it by Mrs. Mann earlier that morning. Sometimes, when it was raining, she left food out even the night before, but she had no wish to draw mice, or rats, or, for that matter, to draw other birds. Only this one, who knew just where to look.

Every day for ten years, the bird came to be with her friend, to stay the day and then to mysteriously go away only to return the next morning. Clearly the

THE BLOCK

bird had a name as well as a personality. Even though Mrs. Mann herself didn't seem to have a first name, the bird did. She called it Pitzi. The bird responded to this name when called by Mrs. Mann. Even when I said her name, Pitzi stood alert, although she did not come directly to me. She gave me the same, or almost the same, wide berth that she gave to everyone, except Mrs. Mann.

One morning, Pitzi just didn't arrive. She never came back again. After such a long time, it could only be presumed that the bird had either died or had been killed in some way. The absence of her feathery friend broke Mrs. Mann's heart. Still, she went on with her required daily chores, including making dinner for her husband and cleaning the hallways and her apartment. But her spirit was broken. She was objectively in good health, and obviously got plenty of exercise climbing five flights of stairs and doing all of the chores assigned her. Yet, not just her spirit, but her heart was broken.

She went on that way for a while, gradually becoming less emotionally involved in her daily life. One evening, when her husband came home, having finished his chores, he found her lying on the couch. She was dead. Now it's true she was a good age, but she was healthy. Her death was a surprise to us and a shock to him. He did what needed to be done and functioned on his own for a few months. But then he proceeded to take active steps to find another companion, another wife. At a time when not only did no one have a television, very few had telephones. At a time when computers were only science fiction dreams for most people and certainly were not in any households, he wrote a letter and put it into the Hungarian newspaper, specifying his wish to find a woman to help him. He listed the characteristics that he would need, such as good character and willingness to work hard.

I was surprised, but with a smile on my face. That's brave, I thought. But some people were shocked. I thought it was a good idea. He was lonely and had been devoted to his wife for all those years. He was so lonely that he couldn't even bring himself to do all the work himself anymore. After all, he was getting older, too.

And he got responses! Two or three women responded. He interviewed each of them, and one was just right for the situation. She was a lovely person. In six months they were married. She was not my Mrs. Mann. There was no special mystery about

THE BLOCK

her. But she was simply a kind and warm person. By this time, I no longer needed a babysitter and was not involved in their lives in any significant way, except as a neighbor. I was glad for him and for her. He had been close and loyal to the first Mrs. Mann, but he still had the capacity, not just for devotion, but for openness and courage and love. He was able to let go of the impossible and live the possible. The better-than-possible, a connected life.

I soon moved out of the neighborhood, while he was still alive. Years later I heard that he had lived well into his late eighties. He died on the job, just as he would have wanted to. His widow—he had married the woman who responded to his ad in the newspaper years before—was permitted to stay in the apartment and to continue her work in the house, doing the cleaning and mopping of the inner part of the house. A new man had been hired by management to do the handyman jobs and supplement her work.

Pitzi never returned.

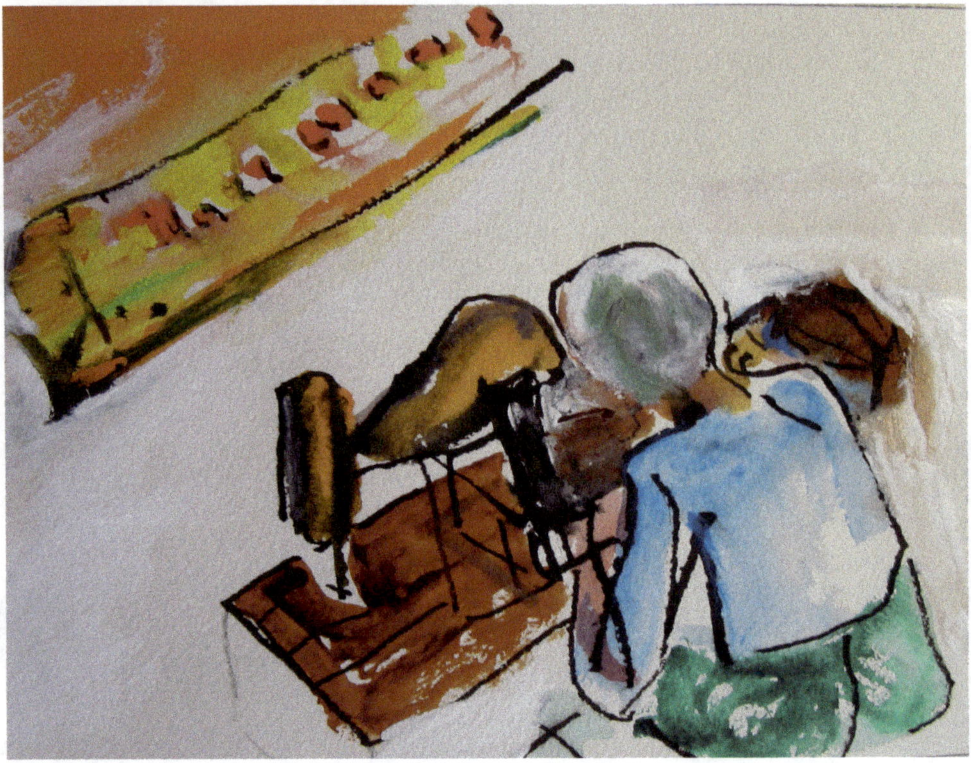

9. Uniforms and Hollywood

I

What does an enemy alien do for a living? Before the time of space exploration, what did it mean to be alien? To be against something. To be from somewhere else. To be different. Even, to be a danger, a threat.

But how is a person with a needle and thread, whose feet are pushing the platform of the sewing machine, frightening? True. As a tailor, the person would have scissors. Perhaps even a small pocket

THE BLOCK

knife, with a two or two-and-a-half-inch blade, to open tight seams.

And of course, a thimble. The all-threatening thimble. The thimble was indispensable to his work, no matter what garment he worked on. Although all thimbles are pock-marked to catch the head of the needle, there are different shaped thimbles. Basically, one kind is covered on top. Looked at upside down, it looks like a small metal cup, just big enough to cover the tip of a small middle finger. Those are generally used by women, often seamstresses who want to protect their nails, or by those who sew incorrectly.

The more professional kind of thimble is shaped somewhat differently. It does not sit on the top of the finger but rather slips down to fit comfortably over the nail for about three quarters of an inch. The metal is cut flat on the top, while the metal bottom of the thimble is rolled slightly to make it smooth and somewhat more secure and solid at the lower part of the fingernail. Unlike the misused thimble, struck on the head of the needle with the top of the finger covered by its metal cap, the more professional thimble, with the opening on top, is struck on its side with the finger crooked slightly in towards the palm of the hand. The sewing motion is from right to left rather than from top to bottom. Since it is much less fatiguing this way, the tailor is able to sew continuously for hours. No need to aim the metal thimble head accurately, but rather just to slide it a fraction of an inch forward with each stitch made. That's true for enemy aliens' thimbles, or for anyone else's, for that matter.

How does someone become an enemy alien? That's simple. All you have to do is go on vacation, get stranded in a country that goes to war, and complicate the matter by being from one of the countries in the enemy camp. It's not necessary to be a soldier. Or a pilot. Or a sailor. Or an officer. Or even a policeman. No, not at all. You just have to be anybody who is stranded away from home and speaks the wrong language and eats the wrong food. By the way it helps to be believed as alien if the clothes you wear are just a little different from those of the people around you. Anything that permits the formation of the idea of an in-group and out-group, of belonging or of being foreign.

Of course, it helps if you don't speak English, don't drive a car, but ride a bicycle instead. And it's even worse to walk long distances. That will surely

THE BLOCK

create interpersonal distance, as well. This general discussion could fit at any time, in some ways, and any tailor. But this is about a particular tailor, Joe.

As a young man in his late twenties, he came to this country to visit his older sisters, both of whom had been here for over a decade and were married and settled into stable jobs and neighborhoods. Seeing that war, world war, was imminent, he really couldn't go home. He got a job in a dry cleaning store and did minor alterations for customers who used the dry cleaning service. As gratis work, he replaced buttons that had fallen off or been lost in the cleaning process. He stitched hems torn in handling, or cuffs that came down after contact with too many other clothes in the cleaning solution. Sometimes more extensive alteration was needed, for example, to let out pants that were too tight, or to pull them in, if the owner had lost a lot of weight.

But this was still the depression, the Great Depression, and people had very little money to spend on niceties. At that time Joe earned three dollars a week and a dozen eggs cost between ten and fifteen cents. Once he settled in a bit, married, and was expecting a child, the couple ate eggs almost every night for dinner, partially because that's all she could keep down with her morning sickness, and partially because it was such an inexpensive source of protein. Later in life they joked that their child had been formed pretty much solely on eggs. The perfect protein?

After Pearl Harbor, full military plans went into effect, not just in the military sector, but in the general economy. Items had to be produced, manufactured, provided to foster the war effort. Soldiers needed uniforms. Officers, in particular, needed well constructed uniforms.

Joe was a skilled tailor. He had passed his final exam in Europe by stitching a suit of woolen clothes (jacket, vest, and two pair of pants) for himself, completely by hand. It had to be a black suit sewn solely with white thread. Not a stitch could be visible.

He was hired, actually conscripted, to make officers uniforms at a large, transformed floor of a fancy department store that had partially become a factory, a clothing factory. Yet each rank had a somewhat different looking outfit, so it couldn't simply be produced, like underwear, on a mass scale. Upscale military officers, both for themselves and for

THE BLOCK

the men they led, needed not only to act their parts, but also to look their parts.

For five years, Joe made uniforms. Working long, hard hours in the department store, become factory, he did his part for the war effort. He and his family lived with the blackouts every night, with rationing of meat and eggs and butter and so much more. In the Automat, sometimes a small amount of sugar was available for tea or coffee, but only as dispensed by a person at a separate table in the middle of the room, who doled out one small spoonful into each cup. Yes. One, and only one, tiny spoonful was permitted. That's of course, when there was any sugar at all.

Cars not only had trouble finding, or simply couldn't find, gasoline. They also could not replace tires that had become damaged. Rubber was crucial to the war supplies. Many parked their cars, if they had them, outside the city and later, simply left them there until the war was over.

Because of the shortage of fabric, since parachutes and other military equipment required fabric, fashions for women became smaller in many ways. Dresses, which is what every female wore unless they worked in a factory, were short without ruffles or extra width in the skirt. Coats had no collars and were definitely not made double-breasted, that is with overlapping fronts. Men's pants ceased to have cuffs, since that was extra fabric, too. Sheer stockings were virtually unavailable. Women wore heavier stockings that were both thicker and warmer than what became the more commonly used nylon stockings after the war. And, after the war, fashions changed drastically. Skirts became very long almost to the ankle, and full skirted. Skimping on fabric was unnecessary in peacetime.

II

Yes, skimping on anything after the war made increasingly less sense. Gradually things changed a lot. Soldiers returned and needed employment. For most of them, preferably a return to their prewar jobs. But by no means was this necessarily possible.

Many women filling these jobs during the war had to be let go to create vacancies for the veterans. Although Joe had not been a soldier, his job, too, was no longer required either by the government or by him as a civilian conscripted worker. He was unemployed. In looking for work, he had to take into account not only what positions were available, but

THE BLOCK

also which ones were suitable to a man of his considerable sartorial skill.

In this postwar shift, his family had moved to an equally small apartment, but farther downtown, to what later became the Upper Eastside. Temporarily, he worked for a small, really a tiny, factory farther downtown, and on the second floor. This work place included a continued ongoing service to officers for their uniforms, since they were still in the process of transition back to civilian life. Also for those staying in the military. This job was partially funded by the government and, when that funding was discontinued, the tiny factory closed. Again, Joe was unemployed.

After that, he looked for work solely in the private sector, preferably where each garment might be different. Disliking tailoring, however good he was at it, he had found that the one redeeming factor of the work was that each piece of clothing that he worked on was different from the previous one.

Because of his interest in chess, he went up to the chess club then on Fifty-Ninth Street off Sixth Avenue, just to look in through the partially open windows at the members sitting seriously at the tables and deeply engrossed in their game in progress. While on his way home, he passed a cleaning shop around the corner. He saw that Mme. Yvette Cleaners was looking for a tailor. The job was his. And he began work next day, and continued to do so for almost thirty years.

Obviously, the location pleased him, because of its proximity to the chess club. Soon it was also to be near the new Chess and Checkers House on the hill in Central Park, not a ten-minute walk from where he already worked. Also in this neighborhood, in the immediate vicinity of the dry cleaning store, were a number of upscale residences and hotels. Many actors, who did not want to be troubled with keeping up an apartment themselves, lived in these hotels, including the one which was across the street from the shop and another which was just around the corner, a little past the Chess Club.

As a consequence, Joe had an entirely different clientele, many of whom were not only wealthy, but well-connected. Hollywood actors and actresses, and also behind-the-scenes people in the movie industry, frequented their local dry cleaner, Mme. Yvette. And when something needed to be done on their clothes, the one who remedied the situation was Joe.

THE BLOCK

He became Joe to them, too, and that stayed with him for the rest of his working life. It is no surprise that sometimes they lost weight or gained weight, or bought something that they were not happy with that needed changing. Under these circumstances, he would need to do a fitting. Doing the fitting there, in the tiny workspace provided for his sewing machine and his chair, buried behind racks of hanging clothes which were either waiting to be cleaned, or were cleaned waiting to be pressed, or were pressed waiting to be bagged up for delivery. To say that the space was small didn't do it justice. And there was nowhere for the customer to change clothes. No room for Joe to simply put his arms akimbo, unless he did so in the direction parallel to the sewing machine.

Fittings came to be done in the home of his clients. He had never seen places like that before. Yes. Even the hotel rooms were completely out of his life experience. Fitting his customers in their familiar environment, enabled them to look and feel comfortable in their clothing. That made them do their best work. His best work fostered their best work. A few of the clients became so attached to him and his work, that it was soon clear that he would need to travel with them, primarily back and forth between New York City and California—Hollywood.

Stefan Draughon

They proposed and negotiated a job for him, based in Los Angeles, where he would be making almost ten times the salary he was taking home in New York. And they would help him find a home for himself and his small family.

When the contract arrived, he needed only to sign it to begin a completely different life for himself three thousand miles west of where he had landed on his first visit to the United States. West of his life as a single man, of his married life, the birth of his child, and his being an enemy alien during the war.

Though he was a United States citizen by now, not only he remembered that time, but so did a number of the actors, directors, and cinematographers he had come into contact with. They had been in that state, too. They knew what that felt like, and they respected the courage with which Joe had not only survived, but had lived during these past ten years. He would be leaving a one-bedroom apartment, overcrowded with sewing machines, remnant fabrics, including linings and canvas for backing lapels, and of course threads and buttons, zippers and snaps, ribbons and needles, scissors and tape measures, rulers and chalk, seam binding, and so much more.

THE BLOCK

No. Leaving the apartment would not have been any great loss in and of itself. His daughter, it's true, had just begun to go to a free and highly-rated junior high school and high school. That might pose a bit of a problem. His wife's family was here on the East Coast. His own family was spread out over the world, though mainly here in the United States no farther west than Chicago. Many relatives in Europe had been killed during the war or just after it. His mother was dead, too.

As he walked in the door that night, with the contract in his pocket, what was for dinner seemed irrelevant. Dinner was best done-with quickly, so they could move on to the issue at hand — the contract. Although his English was not that strong, and none of his friends or family was a lawyer, Joe had shown the contract to another customer at work, who said that it was a normal, unexceptional contract and that the real question was whether Joe wanted to move to the West Coast and to a very different kind of atmosphere and work and life, let alone climate. Joe loved cold weather. His hands were always warm, although he neither owned nor wore gloves.

So, it was not the legality of the contract. No. It was not an issue of whether he was being led astray or taken advantage of. Rather it was whether, having left the large cosmopolitan capital city in Europe to come to the most heterogeneous, cosmopolitan city in the United States, he was willing to move himself, his family, his newly planted roots, yet again, across country to a strange place, where he had never been. Clearly the contract was for five years. What about afterwards? Would he be able to move back east and start all over again back here on the East Coast for a second time?

On the other hand, the salary would be ten times more than he was currently making, and he'd be assured of it, at least for those five years. But, what if he didn't like it there? If they were not kind to him? He could not simply say the truth, as he did here, that he didn't want to work on this garment, or make up some tiny excuse, like he didn't know how to do the task, or didn't have time then with his other commitments. No. If he was unhappy there, he'd be stuck for five years. And so would his family. Basically, the decision to move or not rested with him, since his family had mixed feelings about the move.

Ultimately, his decision not to sign the contract was a renewal of his relationship, not so much with his family, but a re-avowal of his commitment to New

THE BLOCK

York City. Here he was not "alien." This was where he belonged in the world now.

Yes. Whenever he was asked where he was from, in his always-thick accent, accompanied by his broad smile and warm handshake, he would proudly say, "I am a New Yorker."

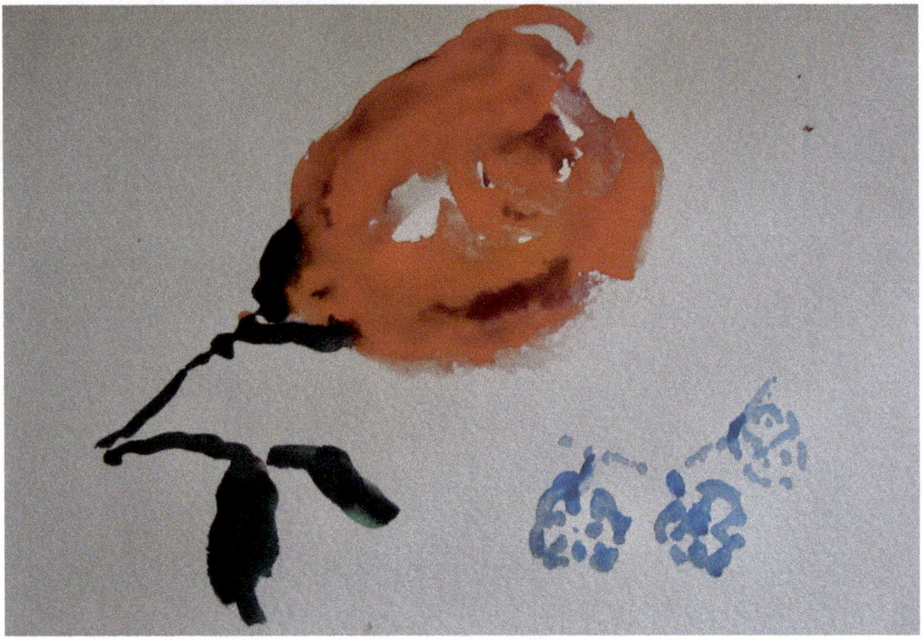

10. A Trinket from China

A trinket from China
A rose from France
Both for Miss Trefan
Long may she dance. (Nora Fox, 1953)

After more than half a century, I can still hear her saying these words to me. How is it that I, who cannot memorize even a few lines of text, have effortlessly recalled these all my life?

THE BLOCK

I

Inside a cube-shaped box was a lavender, carefully-carved, plastic container with a floral arrangement in relief on top and parallel lines surrounding the base of the clam-shell shaped vessel. At the very bottom, there was a lacey carving, resembling a tiny skirt around the base. Inside the box lay a bracelet. From China. Its simple gold-plated, sterling silver chain had twelve small balls suspended, evenly spaced, around the chain. Each three-eighth inch ball was carefully carved in a filigree manner, and each half, top and bottom, unscrewed from the other revealing a small quantity of solid perfume, which added yet another sense to the aesthetic experience of the gift. At the very top of the original box there had been a red silk rose with a card attached by a thin silver ribbon. She presented this to me on my thirteenth birthday. Inside the card, Nora Fox had written her poem by hand, clear and unadorned.

Surely, I had received gifts before in my life. Some of them given with a great deal of thought and caring. But never had a gift meant more to me and never would any other gift mean more than this one. The simple, original beauty of the feeling, of the workmanship, of the person giving me the gift was unique.

Not only was her gift unusual and special, so was she. She looked like no one else I'd ever met and certainly looked like no other woman on the block. Later I found out this had always been the case for her. She was different.

Her mother lived in Pittsburgh, but Nora had left home in her late teens, though staying in the area. Quitting high school, she went for six months to secretarial school and did typing for a living. But her passion was dancing. She studied on scholarship at the local Ballet Academy and was so good that she was singled out for performances there and locally. She quickly found a dance partner, and was never without one after that.

Trying to make a living typing, and dancing the rest of the time, became too hard to keep up, so she and her dancing partner committed to an increasing number of performances at low pay to compensate for the termination of their "regular work." Her long-term stable dance partner, Vernon, and she not only

THE BLOCK

danced well together, they got along well, too. She was in no hurry to form a romantic relationship and was not religious. He was Jewish culturally and gay, preferring short-term relationships with men to any sexually committed relationship then and, in fact, throughout his life.

Once, as a frightened teen-ager, I asked her if she had been lonely for dates with men all her young life as a single woman, she gave me her first big piece of information about relationships and life. "It doesn't matter what you look like," she said reassuringly to the be-pimpled me, "You'll never have any problem having plenty of male company as long as you're not looking to marry them." Even at that young age, and with my insecurity in that area, I instantly knew it was likely to be true. And it was. Never in my life have I lacked for male company or dates. But never did I let myself go into relationships with men with the idea of "hooking" them or "getting them" to marry me.

The freedom that Nora and Vernon gave to each other, the honesty of their relationship with each other, as well as, of course, their compatibility as dance partners, eased their life-long friendship through her marriage to another man decades later, and until Vernon's death a decade after that.

She and Vernon got tired of living performance-to-performance on an unstable income and decided to open a dance school in Pittsburgh. It would permit them to take some performing jobs, as "Nora and Vernon," and give them the opportunity at the year-end recital to perform a little, too.

Their school prospered and lasted eighteen years, until the outbreak of WWII in Europe and the death of Nora's mother. With young people's energy and work diverted to the war effort, dance classes were not high on their "to do" lists.

But there was another reason that the late nineteen thirties was important to her. Her future husband, Mr. Fox, was a German Christian who was against the Hitler regime. He had escaped through France to the United States, leaving behind all his family and property, except for some meager funds. I would tell you his first name, but frankly I cannot remember it. We probably never exchanged more than a few dozen words in all the time he was alive. He was always "Mr. Fox" — Mrs. Fox's husband — and not talkative.

THE BLOCK

Once in New York, he could not find work right away and took any job he could get to help him live simply, except for going to the opera, standing room tickets only, because music, especially German music was his passion.

Since he had been upper-middle class in Germany, he was used to having servants, including a cook and valet. It may sound strange, but once here, a non-citizen and enemy alien and beyond the age of serving in the military, he got the only job he could at a small Midtown hotel for bachelors who needed cleaning services and who found a barber shop as part of the hotel very convenient for haircuts and shaves. It was not fashionable for men to wear beards at that time. And their hair was kept very short. Mr. Fox acted as valet at the hotel, which was easy for him to do, at least in terms of knowing what needed to be done and how, although emotionally it was not simple to be in the reverse role of server instead of served. A short barber school course at night prepared him to cut the customers' hair, too, as the hotel's needs changed, given the number of employees who continued to be drafted.

Even after his marriage, no one really knew him on the block. They would formally greet him, just as I did, as "Mr. Fox." He never went out. After work, he stayed home listening to music, particularly German opera, and mostly Wagner. I never came to fully understand and reconcile his antipathy to the Hitler regime with his passion for Wagner's music. Actually, not never. A half a century later, I can finally see the beauty in that music and not tie it to the twentieth century, but rather to the world of mythology and often to ninth and tenth century Europe. Now I know that then it was the Magyars, the Hungarians, who were militant and conquering much of Europe. They gave that conquest up once Hungary became united under the converted Catholic king, who was later sainted as Saint Stephen. His hand remains a holy relic in a large church in Budapest.

Mr. Fox and Vernon got along well enough so that he continued to be part of their family holiday celebrations as long as he lived. Even after her marriage at forty, Mrs. Fox was possibly the worst and clumsiest cook imaginable. Everything was overcooked or undercooked. And, unlike her precise musical and dance rhythms, nothing was finished at the proper time. The roast had to wait the half hour for the potatoes to cook. And the salad drooped under its vinaigrette dressing prepared two hours before the meal was served. The home was clean and orderly, but food and eating were not a priority.

II

I came into her life as a ten-year-old when she decided to open her dance classes, in part because she missed dancing and in part because her seven-year-old daughter was getting to the age where she needed some instruction to help her be more graceful than she seemed to naturally come by.

I'd never really met Mrs. Fox, but had seen her walking their dog, a good-natured, mostly-white fox terrier with a few irregular black spots. Coincidentally she was called "Lili." I had been "Lili" all my life to differentiate me from my mother with whom I shared the legal first name, "Liliom." How this happened at my birth—how come two adults could not come up with another name for their baby—beats me. But I have always loved the name "Lili" and was actually okay with sharing it with the terrier, independently named. I liked the dog, and it was because of her that I first made acquaintance with Mrs. Fox. I had no idea that she danced.

Mrs. Fox, as everyone called her, rented a space in a church adjacent to our elementary school for two afternoons a week. Classes began at three-thirty in the afternoon on Mondays and Wednesdays in the basement of that church. Her fees were minimal, though, if a family needed to pay less, that was never a problem. What I'm saying is, she never did it for the money. At first, as I said, she did it for her daughter, her calm and passive, very blonde and fair, blue-eyed daughter. Later, I think it's not unreasonable to say, she did it for herself and for me, her young, highly energetic, brown-eyed, olive-skinned, brunette little friend and fellow artist.

The saying is, "We don't pick our parents." Well, they don't pick us either. And it gradually became eminently clear that Mrs. Fox's daughter was nothing like her mother. Neither in appearance nor bodily movement. And not in interests either. As far as I can remember, Alice did nothing of her own volition. She dutifully did her homework, kept quiet so as not to disturb her father's music listening, and she let her mother serve her all the time she was still at home, not in a self-centered way, just as an expression of her passive nature.

THE BLOCK

Mrs. Fox's hazel eyes did not stand out as her dominant feature. Her well-formed body did. Although she was fifty years old when she started teaching again, her body was that of a young girl. Her small frame, shapely but thin, her small well-shaped breasts could have been those of a thirteen-year-old. She neither strove to display them pretentiously nor to hide them. Unlike the bras that the other women on the block wore, which were heavy and boned and removed any hint of nipples being at the tip of the breasts, Mrs. Fox wore bras that were thin and lightweight, revealing the full shape of her breasts, while protecting them from irritation from fabrics or other rough objects. Her simple clothes fit close to her body without being seductive. She managed to appear comfortable with her body and unashamed of it, without being seductive or using it in any way interpersonally. It was just another fact of the world.

Sensible shoes finished off her every-day dress. Even her two pairs of dress shoes were clearly chosen to provide solid support, stability, although they did have two-inch heels. Except for her white-gold wedding ring and engagement ring with a small diamond, she wore no jewelry. At least I never saw any.

At dance class she wore a simple crewneck top and moderately short shorts which looked just right for the situation. She danced before the class relatively infrequently, although she did demonstrate the forms before we did them to help us learn. When we either as a group, or one-at-a-time, crossed the floor, either straight across for a shorter distance or diagonally for a longer one, she suggested corrections to our form. She never put one student ahead of the others by saying something like, "Why don't you do it like Jane?" Instead she would say nothing or pick something the child was doing correctly and comment on that. If the position was not a healthy one for the child, she would take the child gently aside and point out the problems continuing that posture could create.

Expenses for equipment were minimal. Basically, a pair of ballet slippers, and/or a pair of tap shoes. For adolescent girls and boys (over ten years old) she asked that in class they wear a dancer's belt, a wide and heavy band of elastic around the pelvic area, with a soft woven fabric slung under the crotch. Although what we were doing was not so strenuous as to be likely to be of any harm to us, she took no chances with her students. In addition, she personally checked every child's feet once a month to make sure there was no irritation developing and that the toenails were being cut straight across.

No child was allowed to go en pointe in toe shoes until age eleven, and then only after the child had learned the basics of flat work, that is, work at the barre and floor work in pleated-toe black ballet slippers, bought on the smaller and wider side, to which someone had sewn a small piece of elastic across the instep of each shoe to help keep it in place, especially when the toes were pointed.

Once a month, she worked individually with each child. We called this "the stretch." In our ballet slippers, we would, in turn, rest our backs against a wall. Mrs. Fox would then lift our less-limber leg up to a level that was comfortable. Then she would do so with the other leg. Just as people are right and left handed, so they are right and left footed. And the two pairs of extremities are not necessarily in parallel. I am right handed and left footed. That means that lifts and extensions on the left are easier and more comfortably extended on that side than the other. This stretch was done from the front, then to the side, and lastly to the back. Naturally limber students had absolutely no trouble bringing their legs straight up in front of and against their chest. Others could only lift them part of the way, perhaps no farther up than the waist. Going backwards, some could touch their forehead with their toes. Occasionally someone could bring a heel to the forehead. And there was no predicting which bodies would move comfortably and how far by simply looking at them. We loved these stretches because they felt good and also because month after month, we could see the incremental growth in our flexibility and in our capacity to move more comfortably and gracefully.

The four to six-year-olds learned separately, away from the older children. Their work was done on a thick blue mat on the floor. Sometimes it was individually supervised somersaults, or head and hand stands. Other times there was an exercise in which a student would get into a posture and would become a "stack of pancakes." When this pose was taken, then Mrs. Fox would make-believe-pour syrup onto the stack of pancakes, the folded-up child, and the other children would giggle and couldn't wait to be the next candidate for becoming pancakes, with syrup, of course.

After a year of flat work, students were asked to take tap dancing as well. Dancers and some athletes become muscle bound, with lumpy, hard muscles that, once solidly formed, were usually permanent. But, by taking tap dancing simultaneously with ballet, the muscles in the body had a chance to shake out and loosen so that the rock-solid muscles, in the calf for example, just didn't form. Mrs. Fox's legs were well formed even though she had danced all her life, until at age forty-one, when her daughter was born. And she had no bulging muscle forms or lumps.

III

Maybe it was that I had been folk dancing since I was five years old, or simply because I had the necessary body flexibility and awareness to dance well, I quickly rose, so to speak, to the head of the class. When that became clear to everyone, without a word being said, Mrs. Fox talked with me and asked me if I would like to be her assistant. At first, as needed, I could help another student who was having difficulty learning a new step.

Or I could simply take over the class for a moment, should she be distracted by another student or issue. She had already given me free lessons the year before, since she knew that my mother, though willing to pay for weekly, hour-long piano lessons, was unwilling to pay for dance classes. She already believed in me.

Having, herself, begun to work early and having been poor, Mrs. Fox did not believe in unpaid work and would give me ten dollars a month for that help. Today that sounds minimal, but when people were making much less money than now, and a subway ride was a nickel, that really was not a small amount for an eleven-year-old child to begin to earn.

The following year we had another talk, and she insisted on broadening my job description and increasing my monthly earnings to twenty dollars a month. I could now lead the barre work, going through the foot and hand positions at a rod along the wall, usually about three feet high. Or lead the *port de bras*, the arm movements, on the open floor, away from the barre. These activities were in addition to helping individual students having difficulty with a particular movement.

By the time I was sixteen years old, she asked me to teach four-week summer classes for beginners who had no experience. Or for those who felt they needed a little extra attention. During these classes she was not there. I received the small, but full, payment for the lessons. This meant that I had gotten working papers just after my sixteenth birthday, the first working papers I officially had. So, I started my work-life in my first real job, though only for the summer, as a dance teacher. Who knew? Would I follow in her footsteps?

IV

Once each child attained a certain level of skill as a dancer, he or she was granted a solo at the end of the season. Planning each dance routine was not simple cookie-cutter work. Everyone was different. And being "different" herself, Mrs. Fox deeply understood and appreciated that. Actually, she thrived on human individuality. Let me show you how she did this with a few of her students. After all, each child was different, not just me, and each one had her respect. For me she came to add love to respect.

Maggie was highly athletic and physically strong in her body and in her presentation of self. She could do anything en pointe, no matter how much it would make any of the other students uncomfortable if they even tried it once, let alone repeated her turns and jumps en pointe. However, she was not exceptionally graceful and, when she moved slowly, she began to clown instead of becoming lyrical. So, Maggie needed a fast, jumpy sort of routine, with no time for her inner-clown to emerge. Don't get me wrong. She really was funny. But that's not what her Scottish parents, superintendents at a luxury apartment building, would want to see her do on stage as a child at the dance recital.

Ruth, a gentle and quiet Jewish young lady, tried very hard to do well when forming the individual steps, but her body just wouldn't respond. She could move slowly. That's true. But she could never simultaneously achieve a kind of grace. She was extremely short waisted and fairly thick in the middle, without being heavy. With no waistline and none of the svelte form of the typical ballet dancer, grace was not easy to come by. Ruth needed a routine to emphasize her arms moving slowly and gently, while drawing all attention away from her feet and torso, even when she was en pointe.

Then there was Mrs. Fox's daughter, who was completely different. Alice was extremely thin, very fair, and, even as an adolescent, had none of the

THE BLOCK

curves associated with being a teenage girl who was close to being fully developed. She moved tentatively in a rigid style, uncomfortable in raising her hands and arms up to her shoulders, let alone over her head. Being frail, she never was able to be on point. She became a "bluebird" in a feathery, pale-blue costume. She simply and slowly made her way around the stage, occasionally turning around and letting the feathers flutter in her stead. She looked lovely.

Of course, as a Hungarian girl who was a would-be Spanish gypsy, I had my own physical and aesthetic characteristics. Having relatively small, weak ankles, what I could do en pointe was limited. Eventually, I did very little work in toe shoes. But in flats, in those beautiful, pleated-toe, black ballet slippers, given my sense of rhythm and grace and my close relationship to the music and to my emotions, I could cover a range of tempi, styles, and feelings. Slow and fast, playful and serious, flirtatious and innocent. I had a wide range of movements with arms and head, arms and torso and legs moving comfortably together to express the nuances of the music.

Every year, somehow Mrs. Fox came up with new material for each student, appropriate to the current situation. Each year a new costume, for new shapes, for new skills, for at least a dozen individual students. Also for groups of students who were approximately the same age range and skill range.

That was remarkable to me, in and of itself. But most fascinating was that she had developed a form of dance notation, long before it was formally studied and before easy video recording. Her notation system informed her well, and others could get a good idea of what the individual and groups of students were asked to do and to what music, specifically to which recording or which published version of the music was being used.

Prior to any recording capacity for the dance, it had been the custom for one generation of dancers to observe the previous generation and be coached by them, often individually for solo routines. That system provided older dancers, who did not teach their own classes, to find a solid place in the company even after they themselves no longer danced professionally.

The apprenticeship relationships were often warm, caring ones with a shared sense of devotion to their art. Mrs. Fox's and mine certainly was.

THE BLOCK

V

Mr. Fox died unexpectedly, though after a progressively debilitating bout with Leukemia, in spite of his careful and rigid adherence to a "healthy diet." Death, even after a lingering illness, can feel unexpected to loved ones.

Mrs. Fox closed her dance school at the end of the eighth season so that she could give her daughter more attention during the period before she left for nursing school. Alice was going to a three-year, practically oriented, nursing school where she could begin work early in her training. Academic studies were not her strong point. Other students, too, were beginning to think in terms of their future careers and, for some, of going to college.

Once Mrs. Fox had come to this decision, we had another talk, not only about her future, but mine as well. After walking home from class and standing outside, in front of her home, she said, "I've taught you everything I know about dancing. I need to find out if you would like to go on studying dance, and move toward a career as a dancer. If you would like to study further, and wish to consider it as a future career, just as I did, I will help you find another teacher. If, on the other hand, you would rather focus your energies on your schoolwork and your academic future, I would completely understand."

At that time, I was saddened by her departure and by the pressure that, not she, but life itself, was placing on me. Economically, it was necessary for me make a practical decision. I knew that life as a professional dancer was too uncertain, financially. I needed to focus on going to college and getting a bachelor's degree. In fact, I went on to receive multiple graduate degrees.

That was difficult enough, but it turned out not to be the most overwhelming part of her conversation with me that day.

As a child who had been scolded for getting one B+ on a report card with otherwise all A grades, including conduct, I didn't know how to deal reasonably with my personal limitations. My mother felt I did everything wrong. She felt that way about my father, too, except for the way he, as a Hungarian, did the Tango, which she, no dancer herself, approved of.

THE BLOCK

So, there I was at sixteen, hearing an adult admit what my parents, for different reasons, could never admit. It was crucial, and has stayed with me all my life, to see her ability to calmly comment on her estimation of her capacity as a dancer and teacher. To see her openly and courageously confront me with her limitations, while at the same time not putting any pressure on me to make a decision one way or the other.

Later, after a few false starts in actuarial work and chemistry labs, I taught, in one form or another, for almost all of my life. But in that one moment with Mrs. Fox, I learned, by example, never to be afraid to admit my own realistic limitations to others. That was because of the way she made me feel when she spoke out. I was surely even prouder of her after that for trusting me and treating me with respect to make my own decision.

Consequently, with students and colleagues, and even with those in administrative positions over me, it was simple, when it was true, to say, "I don't know." That has been a blessing all my life. And it has enabled me to continue to learn, to be open to new experience, and to fill the gaps in my knowledge as I went along.

Stefan Draughon

VI

Yet, this learning didn't happen overnight. When I was already in graduate school, I visited her on the same block, in the same apartment, two houses up the block from where I had lived. The house I knew so well, no longer existed. It had been torn down in the hopes of being rebuilt during a building boom. But the boom went bust before they got to that piece of property. My girlhood home was now an empty space, the backend of the parking lot from a luxury building a block away.

I was twenty-six years old and living with a man so different from my first husband, from whom I had been divorced for three years. My boyfriend had encouraged me to confront my mother earlier in the day. That afternoon, I did so in her new apartment, in his presence for support. For the first time in my life, I was coming to understand how neglectful and dismissive she had been to me all my life.

During our conversation she tried to deny her part and put the blame totally back on me and on my limitations. I slapped her on the cheek. Not hard. But

THE BLOCK

I had never been able to lift my hand to anyone before, let alone to her. I'd never knowingly fought back or hurt her before, thinking that she must love me and have my best interests at heart. After all, she was my mother. She was not affectionate either, so any physical contact between us was rare, except for her propensity to slap me when she felt I had been "fresh" in my response to her.

I never hit her again. But the ground was leveled a bit more between us, at least from my point of view. I think having my boyfriend there really did give me courage and also intimidate my mother from freely being her usual self. The only time I remember her expressing love for me was in her delirium from kidney failure, a few weeks before she died. When she came out of the delirium, she immediately began to criticize my hair. I knew, right away, that she was back to her usual self and out of crisis.

Once we left her, I couldn't get the events earlier in the day out of my mind. After dinner I "absolutely" had to see Mrs. Fox. Getting her phone number from information, I called about eight in the evening. I knew it was late. I should have done it earlier in the day—or on another day. But I couldn't wait. I needed to see her. She was surprised when I called and a little uncomfortable that she could not prepare for my visit. Still, she agreed. She, too, wanted to see me, whenever she could.

Her daughter, Alice, was married and living away from the city. Mrs. Fox, a non-smoker with emphysema, was living alone in her fifth-floor walk-up apartment. I had to visit her for my own sake, as well as possibly for hers. She was weak and could barely look after herself. She was gracious to me. It was as if we had never been apart. Of course, I had called before I came over, and asked whether she needed me to bring something. She said, "No."

But when I was actually there, I asked again. This time she said, "Could you help me wash my hair?" I was floored. Terrified of hurting her by doing that, of not knowing how to wash a person's hair, the thin hair of a frail person who could hardly breathe or bend over. Whether it was that I wasn't brave enough, or whether it was rational that I truly didn't know how I would do that in the tiny sink in the small apartment without hurting her, I don't know.

For years I could never quite decide what I should have done. I felt guilty about not having been able to give that to her, especially since she'd accommodated

THE BLOCK

my late visit. And then I remembered how desperate I had been for her love that afternoon — for the real love of the real person I was, not some wished-for fantasy mother or child. But then I remembered how she had dealt with her own limitations and honestly confronted and presented them. I took some courage from that.

But today, I do know how I could have safely helped her. Yes. Just today I realized I could have taken two wash clothes and wiped her hair and head down first with a soapy one and then rinsed it with a non-soapy one till she was clean. But it was half a century later that I learned that. She really is still in my life — poem and all.

At the time, she seemed to understand all this and showed as much loving interest and caring for me as ever. She knew I loved her. We loved each other and were powerfully sure of that mutual caring for as long as we lived.

Yes. I can't help thinking that I was the child of her heart, though not of her body. I'm sure she was my beloved mother, in all but the accident of biological chance. And she would have been proud of me that I didn't give up trying to deal with my limitations, even though that solution took so long in coming. And she was unable to physically benefit from it.

Whenever I hear Debussy's *Clair de Lune*, even when I play it on the piano, I can see and hear how she used to play that for me. Her short, slightly squared fingers, always familiar with the notes and the tune, recalled the feeling of the lyrical music she had danced to and helped others appreciate and share.

To this day, I cherish the "Trinket from China" and the verse it came with. But most of all, I continue to feel the love it came with and the capacity to show love that it nourishes.

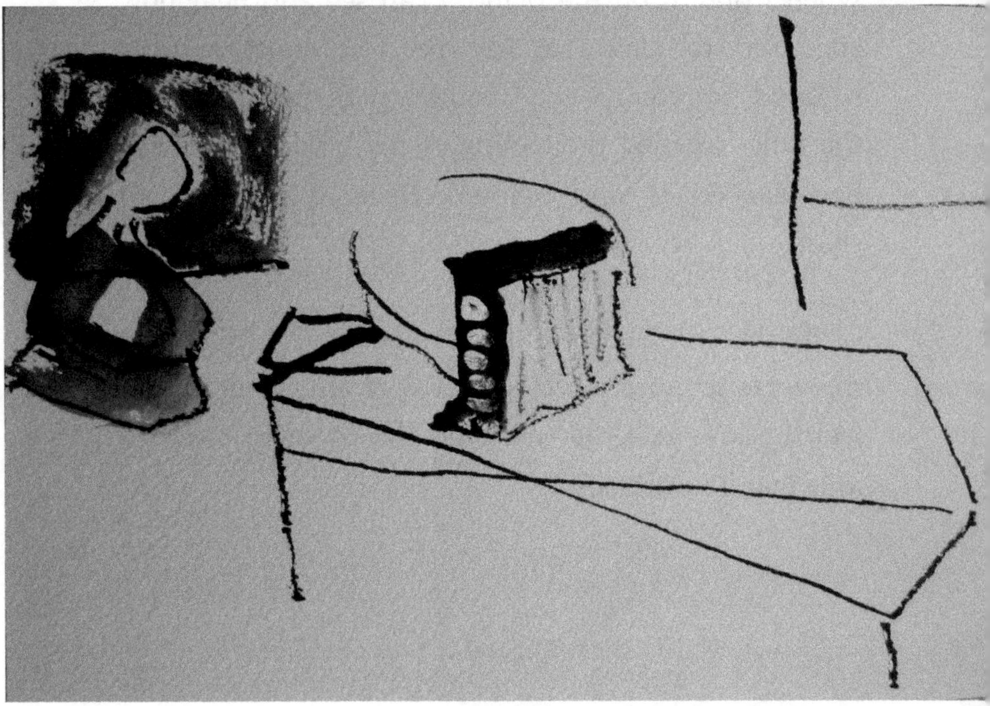

11. The Accordion

The accordion lay quietly on the kitchen table. Rays of sunshine formed striped shadows on its bellows. The keys sparkled like the freshly polished teeth of his dentist.

Hans walked over to its keys and stroked them gently, as he might a beloved dog or child. If only he had been able to touch his daughter tenderly like that, rather than yelling at her because she wasn't perfect, not getting perfect grades at school, not practicing her music enough of the time, and not getting the right sound. She must try harder, take more time to really concentrate. Girls can be so silly sometimes. She was eight now, but he didn't see improvement over the

THE BLOCK

past two years, since she began to take music lessons. Later, it might be still worse.

He picked up his accordion and held it close, as he debated whether to remove it from the kitchen before he turned the gas on. If he removed it, the accordion might survive. Then Helen might just be able to play it in a few years. She had her own smaller accordion now. But growing up is growing up, and her instrument needed to be a grown-up instrument then. Still this one must weigh at least twenty pounds, one third her weight.

Yes. He'd take it to the front room, the room in this railroad flat farthest from the kitchen. Placing it gently on the couch beside Helen's favorite toy, a much-loved stuffed animal in the vague shape of a dog with a long body and short legs. Something like the dachshund. These Americans "cutesify" everything. Fantasy world toys. She would know that he meant it for her — not for her little brother who was only four years old and wanted no part of playing any kind of music. Unless of course, he could play an instrument while he was running around. No, even then . . . it wasn't his style. Yet? Ever? Walking back towards the kitchen, he had to pass the kids' bedroom. Ach! They forgot to fix the bed before going to school. Will they ever grow up and be orderly? All they were asked to do was pull up the featherbed. That's all!

Next, the "master" bedroom, technically, but actually just another small room, in the string of tiny rooms, barely big enough for the double bed. Their home.

He paused a moment looking back at the kids' beds. But he was completely unable to linger on the bed he slept in—the one he had shared with his wife before she died three months ago. He couldn't even fall asleep in it since that time, since she had died. He slept on the kitchen floor, ostensibly because it was closer to the belly stove, the only source of heat in the apartment. He actually was cold at night. The warmth of her body, the sense of her love for him—the only person who had ever loved him. Thinking of that left him chilled. The memory of her was overpowering for him to deal with, even briefly, let alone for a whole night. The kitchen windows. He slowly walked toward the two windows in the kitchen. He made sure they were locked securely. He remembered the small window in the bathroom. That was locked, too.

THE BLOCK

Standing in front of the stove, he paused. He even prayed that he would do this, this one thing in his life, properly. He knew and had well learned that, worse than dying, was failing to die once he tried to kill himself.

"After all," he said to himself, "if you are out of the way, the children would have to move away from this dreadful city, so like Munich in some ways, a large urban city, but not really like Germany."

New York City was nothing like his home as a child and adolescent. He was in many ways the model German child during wartime—physically blonde and muscular, intellectually competent, but also neglected by parents absorbed in the war.

Music was powerful to him in a way that political activity could not be. Everything else was boring. He stayed with it in spite of considerable pressure at school, and from his father at home, to join the German youth movement. As a soldier, a devoted follower of the Third Reich, his father was away from home most of the time.

And his mother? She shared her husband's view. She worked hard at home and volunteered for the war effort, to fold bandages for the soldiers and knit warm socks and sweaters. Every day, every evening, she came home late to wash the dirty dishes that the children had left after finishing the dinner she had provided for them. And then, to start over again in the morning.

One day it was different. Returning home at night, she was shot and killed by sniper fire.

From that moment on, music on Hans's accordion not only took on greater significance for him, it replaced, in its own way, the mother he no longer had.

Yes. Death had been in the atmosphere, in the neighborhood. He had known that. But now, it had been in his home. And surely, in the graveyard beyond the church where his mother lay in the cold and dark—under the ground. He visited her on the way home from school every day.

After requisite school athletic activities at the end of classes and after stopping with his mother, Hans went home to an empty house. His only friend and companion was his accordion, a grown-up one with keys like piano keys on one end of the bellows and

THE BLOCK

buttons on the other end for harmony. Unable to hold his dead mother, he could hold the accordion whenever he wished to. He could touch it with both his hands, feel its pressure on his lap and against his abdomen, feel it in his whole body as its sounds resonated in his soft tissue and bones.

Was he good as a musician? Not the issue at all. The accordion was his friend, portable and huggable. For this sensitive and lonely child, having that, meant a lot. Besides, when it spoke music back to him, and to his silence, beautiful sounds emerged every time. He could no longer imagine life without it. Hans's father arranged, from the front lines, to hire Greta to look after things at home. Her plump, soft body did not feel like the accordion, when she hugged him. But she was a good cook. And she was there!

A tireless walker and devout Catholic, Greta often went on pilgrimages to fulfill her view of what a good Catholic woman does. She began to bring Hans along with her on these walks more frequently and at greater distances from their home in the suburbs of Munich. His developing leg muscles and general strength made it possible for him to walk farther and farther. Besides, he enjoyed it. Sometimes he could carry his small accordion with him and Greta let him play when they stopped along the road in the countryside.

As the war escalated, Greta heard that her employer, Hans's father, was missing in action. Her pay and the funds she received for looking after the child stopped. She decided to stick with her previous plans for an extensive pilgrimage in the direction of the western most part of Germany, near the Swiss border. Silently, with a low profile, she planned to take Hans with her. As usual, they would hike part of the way. Then a bus would take them to the beautiful little church near the Swiss border. She'd been there once before. The bus was scheduled to return in the late afternoon to bring them back home again.

But when the bus arrived at the church, Greta took the boy on an additional hike into the mountains, ostensibly to see the scenery from the mountains. She made sure that they had crossed the border, along the rarely traveled and little-known paths, away from Germany. She lured Hans to walk even farther by permitting him to bring along his accordion. He could play in the mountains, hear the music there as it sounded nowhere else. The instrument fit into his backpack. Greta carried changes of socks and underwear. Since Hans was unaware that they were not coming back, he carried only the accordion and some water.

In the coming years, they traveled together on a long, convoluted path to Geneva and then Southern France. He eventually got passage with the Greta to go to Canada and then to the United States. The rumors of his father's death were no longer rumors. His father had been killed in action. With his mother dead, the orphan-Hans understood he had no one but Greta to rely on. He and Greta settled in New York City, in Yorkville. Their apartment was in the middle of the block, just a few houses down from where that little girl lived, the one who had been molested at school.

After Greta died, he stayed on in the apartment and eventually married a beautiful, blonde woman. She was American, but looked so much like the women he had known in Munich. Only, she was gentle and kind. Quiet and devoted to him — and he to her.

On a routine doctor's visit, under the assumption that she was pregnant again, the doctor discovered she had advanced ovarian cancer. She died a few months after that. Hans was devastated from the time of her diagnosis until her death. It had happened to him again! His mother and then his wife.

Any attempts at maintaining his usual distant and formal manner with his children changed. He became more irritable and stern, even cruel at times. Helen was just like her mother. The guilt that he felt after one of his particularly unkind outbursts towards his daughter eroded any possibility for his regrouping, to focus on building his life on the foundation of his two children and himself. He should have been able to do that. After all, he had a good job, he had a good apartment, not elegant but suitable. But, like a wounded bear, he could find no comfort, physical or emotional, even briefly, so he could begin to rebuild.

As he hated himself more each day, he knew that killing himself was the only way out for him. And there was his life insurance policy. He'd make sure the children were safely at school when he did it. And alert the super to his being away for a while on business.

Images of his former life rapidly passed through his mind as he turned on the gas in the oven. With his beer belly, it was not easy to bend down and put his head into the oven. But he managed.

THE BLOCK

He'd forgotten that there was a pot of boiling potatoes simmering on top of the stove. In the time that it took him to move the accordion to the front room and make his preparations for turning the gas on, the potatoes had begun to burn in the pot and then they caught fire. With the added gas from the oven, the contents of the kitchen exploded. The apartment exploded. The rest of the building was spared. When his children came home from school, they saw only fire engines on the street and smelled smoke. A special kind of smoke. A smell of death, familiar to children in a war zone, but now evident on a block in Yorkville, New York City.

The other children on the block never saw Helen again. No one did. People said she immediately had been taken to her mother's sister in Pennsylvania. "People said." "People said" a lot for a short time. And then, they said nothing.

Helen and her family had vanished from the block.

When the fire department entered the apartment, they noticed the keyboard section of an accordion. It was burned, but with brownish hairs lodged between the keys. No one knew what they were—what they meant. No one understood. Just another piece of trash to be carried away, along with the bathtub on four legs and the remains of the belly stove.

The building never was restored. Instead it was demolished, as was the house next to it and the next . . . until that part of the block—more than half of the block—became a high-rise building . . . like all the others that followed. It replaced the demolished homes of all the people on the block. But no one cared to live in the new building. Besides, they could not have afforded the rent.

It was the death of the block.

The death of a neighborhood.

The death of Yorkville.

And . . .

The Birth of a vastly different Upper East Side.

The End.

Acknowledgements

Without the guidance and help of Peter Arcese and Nellie Beavers, this book would not have been possible. I am deeply grateful to them.

About the Author

Stefan Draughon is Author/Artist of THE BLOCK. Her art work has been exhibited in in solo shows in New York City and in group shows including at the Rhode Island School of Design, where she served on the faculty. Selected recent poetry and paintings, shown together at the Prince Street Gallery in Manhattan in 2016, were published as a book titled, POEMS: And particularly the human face.

Draughon's writing includes a first English translation from the Hungarian of Magda Szabo's novel THE DOOR (1994). She has also written of her experience as an artist in A PASSION FOR WATERCOLOR (2000). Following a staged reading in 2016 in Manhattan, her play, IRREGULAR SHAPES, was published in 2018 as an ebook and print book. The audio version is forthcoming.

www.stefandraughon.com

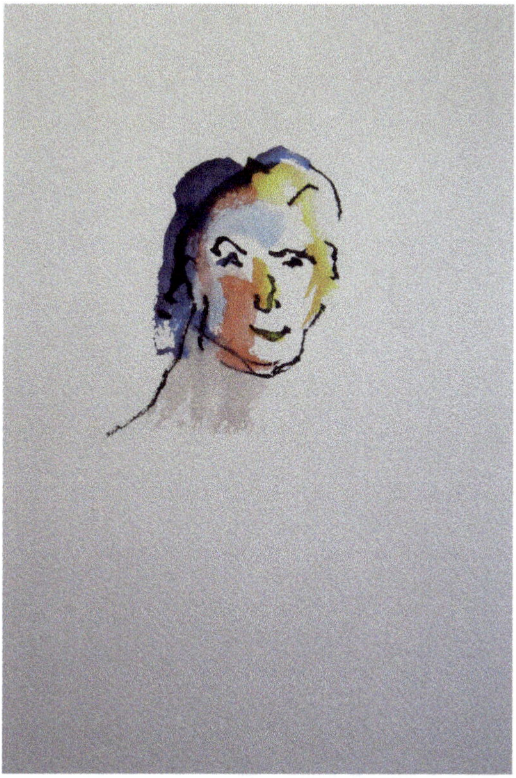

CPSIA information can be obtained
at www.ICGtesting.com
Printed in the USA
FSHW011511240319